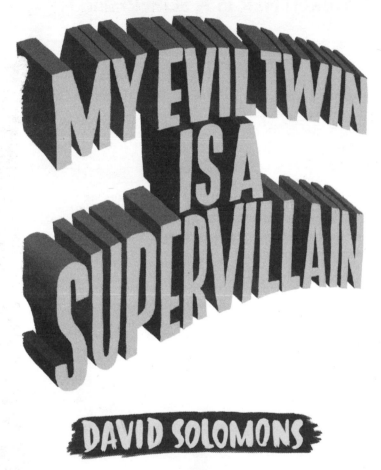

MY EVIL TWIN IS A SUPERVILLAIN

DAVID SOLOMONS

nosy
crow

OUT OF THIS WORLD REVIEWS FOR
MY BROTHER IS A SUPERHERO

"I even think my dad would like reading this book!"
David, The Book Squad, The Beano

"Cosmic! Amazing! Outstanding! Probably the funniest book
I have read for a long time."
Alison A. Maxwell-Cox, The School Librarian

"I was so addicted to it that my mum had to make me put it down."
Calum, aged 11

"Funny, fast moving and deftly plotted, it's the best thing to hit
the superhero world since sliced kryptonite."
Damian Kelleher, Dad Info

"You know a book is going to be good when you're giggling after
five minutes... Ideal for comic readers and superhero experts."
Nicola Lee, The Independent

"An excellent adventure story with real heart that's also properly
funny."
Andrea Reece, Lovereading4Kids

"You'll laugh until you fall out of your tree house!"
Steve Coogan

"A brilliantly funny adventure with twists, turns, crazy characters
and a really hilarious ending. Fantastic!"
Sam, aged 11

"Brilliantly funny."
The Bookseller

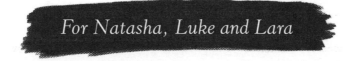

For Natasha, Luke and Lara

In some parallel dimension two of you are voluntarily eating salad, and the other isn't asking me to mow the lawn.

First published in the UK in 2017 by Nosy Crow Ltd
The Crow's Nest, 14 Baden Place, Crosby Row
London, SE1 1YW, UK

www.nosycrow.com

ISBN: 978 0 85763 956 1

Nosy Crow and associated logos are trademarks and/or registered
trademarks of Nosy Crow Ltd

Text copyright © David Solomons, 2017
Cover illustrations copyright © Laura Ellen Anderson, 2017
Inside illustrations copyright © Robin Boyden, 2017

The right of David Solomons to be identified as the author of this work has
been asserted.

A CIP catalogue record for this book is available from the
British Library.

Printed and bound in the UK by Clays Ltd, St. Ives Plc
Typeset by Tiger Media

Papers used by Nosy Crow are made from wood grown in sustainable forests

5 7 9 10 8 6 4

1
MULTIVERSE SCHMULTIVERSE

"Come on, Luke," I muttered to myself as I steered Zorbon's craft past another supernova. "How difficult can it be to pilot a stolen interdimensional spaceship to a parallel universe?"

I sat wedged in the command chair at the centre of a wraparound control panel laid out with a confusing array of touch-sensitive buttons and sliders. A Head-Up Display glowed at eye level showing a moving map of the immediate space around the vessel and a lot of probably very important numbers. Unlike the display, which moved slowly, through the clear bubble canopy stars flew past at an alarming rate. A read-out indicated I was travelling at a speed of 3. Though 3 what, I had no idea.

Swiping Zorbon's keys and "borrowing" his ship had seemed like a good idea at the time. But now as I wrestled with the controls, the words of the universe's greatest smuggler and starship pilot rang in my head. "Travelling through hyperspace ain't like dustin' crops." Years ago, when I'd heard Han Solo speak those words in the first *Star Wars* film, I was puzzled. My confusion arose because I thought Han was referring to an actual person named Dustin Crops.

A light flashed green on the control panel. I was just thinking that at least it was green and not red when the bleat of an alarm reminded me that in Zorbon's topsy-turvy universe red and green were reversed. Uh-oh. I glanced at the floating display. The symbol depicting my tiny craft was heading rapidly towards a big dark circle in space. Now, wasn't there another name for an enormously dark space circle?

Black Hole!

I wrenched the control stick to one side in an effort to miss the giant cosmic dustbin. I felt the craft turn and figures on the display confirmed a change of direction. It looked like I would avoid catastrophe but it was going to be close. I held my breath as I skirted the edge of the gaping hole. Time seemed to slow as I looked up through the canopy into a throat of endless darkness. It was blacker than the Chislehurst Caves I'd begged Dad to take me to when I was little. I was going through one of my periodic Batman phases and wanted to scout out a potential Batcave. Dad led me and Zack to a section he knew where the tour guides never went. Deep underground Dad turned off his lamp, *to give us a little fright*, he said afterwards. I freaked out, but I didn't want Dad to know how scared I was. Somehow Zack sensed my anxiety and found my hand in the dark. Though it was years later, there in the cockpit of the interdimensional craft, I could feel my brother's invisible fingers give mine a reassuring squeeze.

The hull groaned as immense forces clawed at the fragile ship. I could feel it come to a full stop and slowly begin to reverse direction. I was being pulled into the hungry Black Hole. If I couldn't break free of its gravity then my mission would be over before it had even begun. I needed more power. Scouring the baffling control panel my eye fell on a likely symbol. I mashed it with my thumb. There was a pause, then piano music tinkled from hidden speakers and a woman with a weird high-pitched voice began to sing. A message scrolled across the Head-Up Display. It read: Cosmic Classics (remastered). Instead of more engine power, I'd activated Zorbon's favourite playlist. The voice fluttered and swooped like flappy sleeves and just as I was wondering, "What's a wuthering height?" the craft lurched sideways and began to spin. I'd lost control. Recovery systems triggered automatically. The cushioned pads of the command seat inflated, hugging me as tightly as Grandma Maureen when she hasn't seen me for ages, the autopilot assumed control of the flight systems and an oxygen mask fell from the ceiling.

The main drive strained like Dad's old Fiat on a cold winter morning. On the display 3 ticked up to 4 and with a grunt Zorbon's craft shot out of the mouth of the Black Hole. I was free! The command seat relaxed its grandmotherly grip and I sat back with a sigh of relief.

I suspected my destination might be on a list of Zorbon's previously visited stops, and I was right. I tapped the address and let the ship do the rest. As I whizzed across the universe I reflected on my epic journey. I was just like Superman, sent to safety from his doomed homeworld. Except that my homeworld wasn't exactly doomed, and in the comic it's Superman's dad who sends him. My dad didn't know I was gone, not yet. But he would. I wondered if he'd even care. Mum and Dad didn't care about much these days. I pushed the grim thought to the back of my mind, where it could make friends with all the others. There was no looking back – I had to put things right.

Now all that mattered was my mission.

On the control panel a new light flashed. The ship slowed and came out of hyperspace. Suspended before me in the darkness of regular space lay the third planet, Earth.

But not my Earth.

Adjusting its spin, Zorbon's craft entered the atmosphere and blew a futuristic space raspberry at mankind's finely tuned UFO detection systems. The Head-Up Display indicated that a cloaking device had been activated to deal with any nosy radar sweeps. The hull glowed hot and the whole craft shuddered as it skimmed the upper air. It continued its descent, knifing through low cloud to emerge over land. It was night, but a label on the display confirmed my position above the United Kingdom. A few minutes later I was circling over the south-east corner, but as I homed in on my ultimate destination there was a bang from somewhere deep inside the ship and it dropped so fast my stomach was left five hundred metres above.

"Auto-landing failure," cooed the ship's central computer. "Switching to manual control."

The virtual control-stick pressed itself into my hand. Land the ship?! At that point an ordinary person might have panicked. But not me. I wasn't merely Luke Parker, schoolboy and comic-book fan.

I was *Stellar*!

Granted superpowers by Zorbon the Decider to fight for truth, justice and ... well, probably not to steal his spaceship. But anyway, I had powers. In fact, if I'd wanted to I could've pulled the eject lever and flown to earth under my own power. But I needed the ship – it was essential to my plan. Using a combination of regular flight controls, telekinesis and my natural brilliance I steadied the craft and prepared to set it down. I identified an out-of-the-way landing spot deep in the woods, far from prying eyes, the sort of place even a random dog walker would never stumble across. And by that I don't mean that the dog was random, like a collie crossed with an envelope, I mean— Actually, never mind.

As I prepared to touch down a gust of wind lifted one corner of the ship and before I could correct it the opposite corner had touched the treetops. Before I knew what was happening I was cartwheeling through the air towards a large structure illuminated by multiple spotlights. Through the spinning canopy I glimpsed some kind of warehouse. Just before we crashed against it, the ship did this weird dimensional sidestep and ghosted through the roof without smashing it – or me – to pieces. At the last possible second alien safety systems re-engaged, bringing us to a controlled stop.

I popped the canopy and jumped out. The ship's emergency lighting flooded the immediate landing area. I seemed to have arrived in someone's bedroom. At least, it looked like a bedroom, but something felt off. For a start no one was here. Not that they hadn't yet come to bed, it looked as if no one had ever slept here. It was then that I noticed all the other bedrooms laid out around an open corridor and a bunch of labels with weird alien names. In a flash I knew where I was.

"IKEA," I mumbled.

From inside the ship I heard the onboard computer's voice once more. "Activating environmental stealth mode."

The ship began to change shape, transforming from its classic saucer-with-legs outline into a stylishly minimalist bedroom set. In seconds it had morphed into a bunk bed, a modular sofa and a storage unit in lime green.

"Flat pack achieved," declared the computer, which was now a bedside lamp. I knew it was the lamp because every time it spoke the light would flash. I could have sworn that the computer's voice sounded different too. Like a detective from one of those Scandinavian TV shows Mum and Dad were always watching. Which made sense since it was trying to fit in to its surroundings. I had to admit that it was a brilliant disguise. No one would ever notice an extra bedroom in IKEA.

With the ship safely concealed I made my way out of the store to the nearest road. I shivered in the cold night air and took a moment to look up at the stars and reflect on my journey. I'd come a long way. The universe was a big place, but the multiverse was incomprehensibly bigger. Infinite, in fact. Universe upon universe, floating forever in the darkness. It was why I had risked all to travel here. That, and comics. They had taught me that in the multiverse everything is true. From planets made of cheese to civilisations where the dominant lifeforms are hyper-intelligent unicycles, worlds where dinosaurs still roamed, to worlds where everyone is a cowboy (and rides a dinosaur), anything that can be imagined existed out there, somewhere. I was counting on it.

For instance, at that very moment not far from where I stood, my family lay asleep in their beds. A parallel version of my family, leading different lives: Mum, Dad, Zack and me. I scanned the road ahead.

It was time to go and wake myself up.

2
HE'S NOT AN EVIL ROBOT IMPOSTER

"I sincerely hope The Avengers do not show up," said Serge, looking round the tree house, "as we are dangerously low on quiche."

He made a good point. Not about the quiche, but he was right about one thing. The tree house was crowded with superheroes, all chatting to each other about how super they were, while enjoying a finger buffet.

In one corner munching a sausage on a stick stood Star Lad, aka my big brother Zack Parker. Next to him Dark Flutter, otherwise known as my friend and neighbour Lara Lee, sipped sparkling apple juice from a plastic champagne flute. And finally there was Stellar, whose real name was Luke Parker. Yes, I know, that's my name too. Bear with me, as this gets a bit *multiverse-y*.

The Luke Parker on the opposite side of the room came from another, nearly identical Earth that existed in a parallel dimension to ours. From what I could understand of the complex science involved, he and I were basically the same person – being born, growing up, doing all the same things – until a fateful decision caused our paths to split. And what changed everything?

An unfortunately timed call of nature, that's what.

I went for a wee and missed the most important five minutes in history, when a trans-dimensional alien called Zorbon the Decider visited the tree house and bestowed my big brother with powers. Precisely the same thing happened on the parallel Earth, with one crucial difference.

The Other Luke held it in.

Which meant he was still in his tree house when Zorbon popped round to hand out superpowers. In his world *he*, not Zack, was the one who became Star Lad. *Stellar*. In his world he prevented the planet-crushing Nemesis asteroid from destroying the earth. And now he was here. In *my* world.

"Good one," Zack roared with laughter, clapping Stellar on the back. "You're so funny."

I ground my teeth together until they squeaked. The Other Luke had only been here twenty-four hours but I was already sure about one thing.

I didn't like him.

For a start he refused to be called Other Luke, or Luke Two, or Super-Annoying-Luke, claiming that he was the original and if anyone should be footnoted to avoid confusion it ought to be me. The cheek! Unfortunately, I seemed to be the only one with an issue. Zack thought he was simply *hi-lari-ous*, Serge was fanboy-ing over the new superhero, as usual, and Lara was already lining him up for an interview in the school newspaper. Worst of all, they just assumed that Luke-Out-Here-Comes-Trouble and I must be best buds since we were pretty much the same person.

Serge appeared at my shoulder, holding a silver tray piled with some kind of breaded fishy things. He had proposed the welcome party for the new arrival and taken it upon himself to provide the catering.

He shook his head in wonder. "How did the world suddenly become so full of superheroes?" He thrust the tray under my nose. "Sole goujon with mango and lime dip?"

"No, thanks." I pushed it away. "And what *is* that music?"

"It is my Serge Gainsbourg playlist." He prodded the volume control on the portable Bluetooth speaker. "He is my namesake."

Serge appeared to be named after some bloke who sang like he was gargling with gravel-filled mouthwash. *My* namesake was refilling Lara's glass and launching into yet another side-splitting anecdote that involved him singlehandedly saving the world. The *other* world.

I sidled closer to Serge and whispered, "Are we quite certain he's not an evil robot double?" It was a reasonable question. We'd barely had time to catch our breath since running into a cyborg imposter in the course of thwarting an alien invasion last month.

Serge sighed. "We have been through this, *mon ami*; he is the real thing."

I bristled with indignation. "I beg your pardon?"

"*You* are the real thing, of course," stuttered Serge. "But he is *also* the real thing."

I grunted and stuffed a goujon into my face. "Well, what's he doing here? All we know is what he's told us: that Zorbon the Decider dropped him off. What are we now – a superhero crèche?"

Serge sighed. "I am perfectly confident that some world-shattering event will be along presently, bringing with it yet another interlude of horror, anguish and indigestion. But perhaps first we could take a brief moment to enjoy the buffet."

I watched him cross the room and offer round the tray. Hey-Luke-At-Me continued to impress the others with his fabulousness. At one point Zack was laughing so hard he choked on a pizza whirl and Stellar had to use his telekinetic power to dislodge it. They carried on talking shop, comparing cape lengths and discussing which was better – a full-face mask or one that covered just the eyes. Lara was explaining how she could control most small animals, except for cats. No one could control cats. Then she organised everyone into a line and took a photo with the new phone she got after her parents split up.

The break-up had just happened. She and Cara were still living in the house on our street but her dad had moved out. Lara said it had been coming for a long time, but she was still really upset. I told her it could've been worse. When Scarlet Witch and the Vision broke up, his mind was wiped, she went bonkers and they discovered their twins were pieces of a demon's soul. I think that helped put things in perspective for her. And at school I knew loads of kids whose parents didn't live together. What's more, as far as I could make out, there was an upside. While I wouldn't like it if my mum and dad decided to go their separate ways, when George Barton's

13

broke up, he got an iPad. Judging from Lara's shiny new smartphone there seemed to be a pattern involving separation and high-end electrical goods.

Lara marshalled Stellar and the others for one more snap. The three super-buddies and Serge hadn't seemed to notice my absence. Which was understandable, since there I stood in the middle of the group, being funny and charming. Me. Not-me.

My greatest wish in the world was to become a superhero – and it had come true. Right wish, right person. Just the wrong world. This was so weird.

"This is so weird," said Luke-What-Schrödinger's-Cat-Dragged-In. "Hey, Other Luke, don't stand there vibrating like a sad electron. Get over here and join the party."

Now *he* was calling *me* Other Luke? He'd gone too far. Whose parallel dimension was this anyway? "If I were an electron then as part of a quantum field I could effectively be in two places at once," I sneered. "So I could be standing here outside the party, and also over there with you. At the same time."

There was a long silence. I imagined the others were being impressed by my brilliant comeback.

"Well, you kind of are," said Stellar with a broad grin that displayed two rows of shining white teeth.

Toothpaste was clearly more advanced in his dimension.

"Show-off," I muttered under my breath, and grudgingly made my way over.

"Stand there," ordered Lara. "Serge, you too. I want a picture with everyone."

I shuffled up next to the others as she positioned her phone for a high-angle group selfie.

"Not too close, Other Luke," Stellar warned. "You and I must be very careful *never* to touch one another. We are already stretching reality to breaking point by existing in the same dimension. We're like matter and antimatter. I'm obviously matter. Please keep your distance, for the sake of all reality."

I'd expected something like this. In comics and films it's a common problem. When matter and antimatter touch it usually causes the end of the universe or something equally dire.

There was the snap of a shutter as Lara took the shot and inspected the photograph. "Nice."

Stellar reached for a canapé from Serge's tray. "Merely brushing against one another will trigger the collapse of stars and lead to the end of everything as we— Oops!"

He tripped over his cape and fell towards me. Instinctively I flung out my arms. Next thing I knew we were in an embrace, arms wrapped round each other,

15

identical noses pressed together.

"Aaah!" yelled Serge, dropping his tray with a clang. "It is the end of the world. Then with my final breath I must confess my true feelings." He turned to Lara, dragging a hand across his sweating brow. "Lara Lee, aka Dark Flutter, I have something I must tell you. Before the stars go out for the last time, let me declare that I lo—"

A snigger burst from Stellar's lips. Serge's declaration came to a crashing halt, much like an intergalactic cruise liner hitting a space-berg.

"Sorry," mouthed Stellar. "Couldn't resist."

I pushed him off me. "That wasn't funny. You don't joke about apocalyptic singularities."

Zack was trying to pretend he disapproved, but he couldn't keep a straight face.

"It is not the end of the world?" said a small French voice. Serge was sinking fast. And there definitely wasn't room on this life-raft.

Stellar straightened his cape. "Not today, *mon ami*."

In the embarrassed silence that followed, the only sound was Serge's namesake crooning from the speaker.

Serge bent to collect the spilled canapés and Lara helped him clear up the mess. I couldn't help notice that they studiously avoided each other's gaze.

"I think it's time I told you why I'm here," said Stellar, striding into the centre of the room. "I need your help," he declared.

"Well, you've come to the right place," I said, pleased at last to be able to demonstrate my usefulness. "We are S.C.A.R.F., the Superhero Covert Alliance Reaction Force. And we're in the business of—"

"No, not *your* help," said Stellar, cutting across me. He fixed Zack with a long look. "Just *yours*." Stellar planted his feet shoulder-width apart and put his hands on his hips. "My world is in peril. Only by combining our superpowered forces can we hope to overcome the evil might of Gorgon the World-Eater." He extended a gloved hand towards Zack. "Come with me, Star Lad; help me save my world."

Zack pulled at an ear. "Um, yes, of course. Absolutely. But I don't suppose it can wait? It's just that I've got exams. They're only mocks, but…"

I cast a disbelieving glance at my brother. What kind of way was that for a superhero to behave? When Batman sees the Bat Signal he doesn't say, oh hang on a minute I'm just finishing this jigsaw.

"It can wait," said Stellar.

"It can?!" I blurted.

"Oh yeah," said Stellar with a wave. "You can't rush

into confronting a thirty-storey tall megademon with superpowers. We need time to plan. And according to my latest intelligence report, Gorgon is massing his forces in his hidden base. He won't be ready to strike my world until…" He sent Zack a questioning look, as if my brother would know.

"Saturday?" suggested Zack.

Stellar nodded firmly. "Yeah. Saturday first thing."

"You'll miss Dad's comic-shop opening," I said.

Zack shrugged. "Then I'll have to miss it. Nothing is more important than saving the world."

"Except your mocks," I muttered. Zack was taking maths, physics and chemistry early. Did someone say super-show-off?

"If you did want to stay for the opening," said Stellar, "we could probably leave right after and still be back in time to defeat Gorgon the World-Eater."

He made it sound as if they were trying to make a swimming lesson, not confront a world-eating monster.

"Only if you're sure," said Zack.

Stellar nodded again. "The more time we have together strategising the better, right?"

The two superheroes grinned at each other. Decision made, the two of them immediately began devising their plan.

"I think better when I fly," said Stellar. "Shall we?"

With that they bounded out of the tree house, leaving the rest of us standing around with little to say and a lot of uneaten canapés. Typical. Stellar looked like me, sounded like me, but was as annoying as my big brother.

3
THE ROAD NOT TAKEN

"Stellar is clever, *non?*" It was the Monday after the welcome party and Serge and I were back at school. He seemed to have forgiven Stellar for embarrassing him in front of Lara, and had slipped in to his default state of fanboy excitement. "Put yourself in his shoes for *un moment.*"

I frowned at my best friend. Really?

"Ah, *desolé.*" He reached into a pocket for a packet of Fruit Pastilles. "But imagine: you are Stellar, pitched against the evil that is Gorgon the World-Eater, a deadly foe with eyes and ears everywhere." He paused. "I do not mean to suggest that the deadly foe's body is covered with eyes and ears in some sort of terrifying mutation, only that he has a highly efficient intelligence network."

"Yeah, I got that."

"So, how do you outwit such an all-seeing enemy? From where do you recruit an ally? *A completely different universe*. Such brilliant strategic thinking, do you not agree?"

I did agree, but that didn't mean I had to say so aloud. Stellar's brilliance wasn't something I had any wish to celebrate.

"It is just the sort of superior plan that you would come up with."

I smiled at the unexpected compliment. It was weird being best friends with someone who won't stop gushing about your trans-dimensional superhero double, so it was good to hear he hadn't forgotten that Stellar and I were different people. Even if we were also the same person. This quantum entanglement stuff made my head hurt.

"But did you really buy that business about Gorgon the World-Eater?" For a terrifying global threat, Stellar had been remarkably relaxed about the timescale. And there was something about the stupid name. It teased a distant memory that I couldn't pin down. "What kind of name is that anyway? I bet he doesn't actually *eat* worlds."

Serge thought for a moment. "It is possible that he calls himself Gorgon the World-Eater not for any concurrence with a particular set of superpowers, but simply because it is a chilling name. There are many similar examples. Doctor Doom, for instance, whom you never see interrupt his evil plans in order to spend a morning writing prescriptions at the local GP surgery. Fruit Pastille?" Serge offered me the packet and I took one.

"Stellar's so full of himself," I said, chewing the sweet. "Now, if *I* had superpowers…" I caught Serge's eye and felt myself run out of steam. We both knew the end of that sentence had already been filled in, and it was temporarily sleeping in my tree house. Stellar was camped there, safely out of sight. I'd lent him a spare house key so he could nip in and use the toilet, figuring if he happened to bump into Mum or Dad they'd think he was me.

The school buzzer sounded and we plodded off to our next classes. Phoebe Warren strolled past stroking a guinea pig, followed by Edouard Galliard carrying a stick insect in a glass case. It was Pets In School week, and the whole place was one squeaking, barking, mewing, clicking petting zoo. I didn't currently have a pet. My last one had been a gerbil when I was six years old. He'd had a tan and white coat and distinctive black marks over his eyes like a superhero mask. I'd named him Wayne and spent all my birthday money on him, filling his cage with a gerbil wheel, a climbing frame, his own special tunnel habitat and even a pet-powered car. I was training him to be the gerbil equivalent of Batman. I also wanted him to live forever and have laser eyes. I missed Wayne.

Serge and I paused outside the stairwell that led to the science corridor. "Are you coming over to the shop later?" I asked him.

The shop in question was Crystal Comics, formerly owned by supervillain turned saviour of Earth, Christopher Talbot. He had sacrificed himself in defence of the planet, and left me his shop. At least, he'd meant to. In reality, what he'd left were three months' unpaid rent and a stockroom full of comics that technically the bank owned. My dad had dealt with Barclays and was now in the process of fixing up the shop for its grand reopening this weekend. Every spare minute I had I was helping out.

"Of course," said Serge. "Where else would I be?"

"I thought you might prefer hanging out with Stellar."

"It is true I plan to check in on him at lunchtime." He patted his bulging schoolbag. "I have a beef bourguignon and a very nice bottle of grape juice."

We agreed to meet up after school, and then I went to my English class and Serge headed off for an hour of physics teaching that now seemed doubtful at best, its basic principles having been blown out of the water by the existence of the occupant of my tree house.

English wasn't on much more solid ground. We were reading this poem written by Mr Freeze, or Frost, or some name like that. It's about a man in a wood who I think is lost. The poem doesn't tell you how he got lost in the first place – was he marooned on a far-flung planet while being chased by a tribe of alien hunters? Was he a highly trained spy with amnesia? It's a bit vague on those points. Anyway, he comes across two paths and has to choose one. Our teacher, Mr Bonnick, asked the class if we thought the man had chosen the wrong path. I said if it were a videogame it wouldn't matter, since there'd be a save-point and if you did choose the wrong path you could go back and try again.

I learned that in this respect poetry is not like a videogame.

My mind drifted back to Stellar and I raised my hand again. I added that if you were part of a quantum field so that you were effectively two people then you could choose both paths at the same time. Mr Bonnick hadn't thought of that.

I wondered how Stellar was getting on in the tree house. I'd left him a stack of comics, but he'd read them all before. He said they had exactly the same comics in his universe, except there Superman is an aardvark. Then wouldn't he be Superaardvark, I'd said, and Stellar had grinned. He was pulling my leg. Again. In quantum physics it seems you can pull your own leg.

When the lesson finished I sprinted to the door with the rest of the class. From behind me I heard a voice.

"Hey, Luke. *Mate*."

I turned to see the figure of Joshpal Khan, weaving through the crowd. Josh used to torment me at every opportunity, but since discovering I was best friends with his idol, Dark Flutter, he'd changed his tune. I think he was hoping I'd introduce him to his superhero crush.

"You going to lunch, *cuz*?" he asked, eyes wide.

That was another thing. One of Josh's cousins had recently married one of mine, which to my horror meant that we had become distantly related. "Uhh…" I hesitated. I was due to meet Lara in the cafeteria – she wanted to discuss some important S.C.A.R.F. business.

The last thing I needed was Josh tagging along.

"Great," said Josh. "I'll come with you."

Clamping a hand on my shoulder, he propelled me from the classroom and along the corridor. He was like some kind of bodyguard, pushing people out of my way, barking orders to make space. When we reached the cafeteria I'm pretty sure he would have tasted my food if I'd asked him. The meatloaf *did* look dodgy.

"What's *he* doing here?" Lara whispered as Josh banged his tray down beside us and pulled up a chair. I could only offer an apologetic shrug. Our S.C.A.R.F. meeting would have to wait.

Josh scraped his chair closer to mine. "So, Luke-*a-saurus*," he said, leaning in and lowering his voice. "Seen much of *You-know-who* lately?"

"You mean Dark Flutter?"

"Shh," he hissed, gesturing over his shoulder. "Don't want everyone to know."

Lara pretended to fiddle with her phone. Naturally, Josh had no idea that she was Dark Flutter. If he'd thought about it he might recall never seeing them both in the same room at the same time, which is often a giveaway in these situations, but Josh wasn't the most observant of people. One thing had become obvious: I wasn't getting shot of him over lunch.

"She called you Commander," he whispered. "Said you were leader of something called … M.I.T.T.E.N.S?"

"S.C.A.R.F." I corrected him. Josh had walked in on us at the golf club as we prepared for our last do-or-die mission to save the earth. He'd seen too much, which made him a security risk. If we were another kind of organisation, say like SPECTRE, we'd get rid of him by inviting him to our undersea headquarters then pulling a lever and dropping him into a tank full of ravenous piranha fish. But we didn't have undersea headquarters or a tank full of piranhas. And when I'd asked the man at the local tropical fish shop if he had anything that would devour a medium-sized eleven-year-old in under a minute he just gave me this funny look and tried to sell me a guppy.

"Yeah, yeah, that was it – S.C.A.R.F," Josh enthused. "Hey, did you see that UFO a coupla nights ago?"

"Uh, no. Must've missed that one."

"How could you, man! Bright as a comet. Looked like it was coming down outside town. Isn't that the sort of thing your S.C.A.R.F. thingy should be investigating?"

"Possibly," I said.

He clapped me on the back, knocking the wind out of me. "Great! So tonight how about we go hunting for little green men from outer space?"

I caught my breath. "Josh, S.C.A.R.F. is a highly secretive and selective organisation. It's for superheroes only. Sorry."

It seemed Josh wasn't used to rejection. His nostrils flared and he crushed his yogurt pot in one hand. "So how come they let *you* in, eh? What makes *you* special?"

I'd talked myself into a corner. I couldn't fly, didn't have a range of spectacular powers like my brother, and I couldn't even command a supremely willing squirrel like Lara. Nor was I technically a sidekick, since in comics they have their own powers. No, I wasn't special in any way. Thankfully at that moment Serge sat down next to me, looking flustered.

"Steve!" bellowed Josh, distracted by Serge's arrival.

Following a misunderstanding at the start of the school year, Josh thought that Serge's name was Steve, and no one had corrected him. Until now.

"His name is Serge," said Lara flatly.

"*Nah*, don't be daft," said Josh, embracing Serge in a friendly neck hold, pressing a knuckled fist into his scalp. "He's Steve. Steve-y. Steve-*in-cible*."

Serge was trying desperately to say something, but Josh's amiable choke-hold prevented him from getting the words out.

Lara squared up to Josh and fixed him in the eye. "Let

him go."

Instantly, across the dinner hall there was a series of small thuds as, at the sound of Dark Flutter's voice, various pets released their grip on their owners and hit the floor.

"All right, all right, crazy-eyed-girl." Josh pushed back his chair and stood up to leave. "Didn't meant to hurt your *boyfriend*. See you later, Steve." He pointed a finger at me, sighting along it like a sniper rifle. "And, Luke *cuz*, I'm joining your club."

"I'll send you a membership form," I said through a fake smile. There wasn't a form, and even if there had been I certainly wouldn't be posting one to him.

Lara moved closer to Serge. "You OK?"

He rubbed his neck. "*Oui*. But only thanks to you."

They gazed into each other's eyes.

"I don't think Josh would've actually strangled you," I said. "I think that's just his way of showing he likes you."

Lara gave a tut of disapproval.

I poured Serge a cup of water and slid it along the table. "What are you doing here anyway? I thought you were going to see Stellar with your fancy beefburger?"

"That was indeed my plan, *oui*. However, I was distracted."

29

"By what?"

"Evie Oliver, Bella Coy and the Quinn twins." Serge took a sip of water. "They were talking in a huddle and I could not help but overhear. A rumour is circulating about the identity of Star Lad. I heard them say that he attends our school."

"Is that all?" This sort of thing was nothing new. Ever since Star Lad's appearance on the scene, every school in Bromley had at one time or another spread a rumour that his alter ego was one of their pupils.

"You do not understand," said Serge, shifting in his chair. "They are saying he is your brother."

4
SPACE GERBIL IN THE FORBIDDEN ZONE

"This is a disaster." Zack sat at the desk, holding his head in his hands.

It was later that same afternoon and I'd found my brother deep in the peculiarly dark heart of the school library. With its dusty aisles and shadowy corners, it was the sort of library where you wouldn't be surprised to stumble across a choir of dead-eyed little kids singing about a nameless horror in the junior fiction section.

"I wouldn't call it a disaster," I said in my most soothing voice. "It's a hiccup." I paused. "A hiccup with potentially catastrophic consequences, I grant you."

"What are you on about?" Zack looked at me with

a puzzled expression. "I'm talking about this." Set out before him on the desk was a printed document about five centimetres thick. He aimed a miserable flick at the top page. "I have to do a risk assessment for Star Lad."

"What's a risk assessment?"

He turned to the first page and read along a row of headings. "*What are the hazards? Who might be harmed and how? What action is necessary?*" He tipped his head back and gave another groan. "There are like a thousand questions and I can't get out of it – it's council policy."

"But you don't work for the council."

"No, but my Star Lad signal is on the roof of the Civic Centre and I need a permit for flying in a built-up area. Oh, and apparently my telepathic powers ought to be registered for Data Protection."

Grumbling, he returned to the document. As he struggled to answer a question in four parts about slipping hazards I filled him in on the Star Lad rumour circulating the school.

"Oh, that's just great." He pinched the bridge of his nose like he was getting a headache. "So now on top of filling out stupid forms I have to deal with a bunch of whispering schoolkids pointing fingers and making snide comments. And what if one of them goes full Sherlock and discovers that the rumour is actually true?"

"That won't happen," I said. "No one's ever going to believe that *you're* Star Lad."

"And why not?" he snapped.

"I'm sure it'll just blow over." I said, swiftly changing the subject.

Zack sighed and put down his pen. "Y'know what, maybe I should go with Stellar right now. Maybe in his world I'll actually be *appreciated*."

It was clear that Zack was getting fed up with his Star Lad duties. "Nobody said that being a superhero would just be rescuing orphans from burning buildings," I reminded him.

He jumped up and slipped on his blazer. "I don't know why people always use that as an example. I've been doing this a while now and I haven't met a single orphan." He tucked the risk assessment document under one arm. "Have you talked to Lara yet? She's furious that you didn't ask her to be on the Gorgon the World-Eater mission."

"Me?"

"Not *you* you. The other you."

That's what Lara must have wanted to discuss over lunch. "Why doesn't Stellar want her?" I asked.

Zack was in a hurry to leave. "I don't know. Maybe there's already a Dark Flutter in his world."

33

Strange. If I was assembling a team of superheroes to take on a megademon, I'd want to recruit as much firepower as possible.

"I have to go and meet Cara," said Zack.

He was crazy about Lara's sister, Cara. Thanks to a run-in with an evil cyborg double, she'd recently broken up with Matthias, her long-term boyfriend and Viking, which in Zack's head had created an opening for the position. Of boyfriend, not Viking. Unfortunately, to her Zack was just the slightly weird neighbour who lurked behind her in the lunch queue and tutored her in physics.

He turned a corner and was gone. As I stood there alone I became aware of the distinctive smell of hot chips. Eating was forbidden in the library, which meant that someone was breaking the rules big-time. Curious to meet the offender I followed my nose down the aisle, but before I had reached the end I stopped in surprise. A figure blocked my path.

Stellar stood with his back towards me. He was wearing my spare school uniform. Which meant he must've gone into my room to get it. The cheek.

"What are *you* doing here?" I whispered. "Were you following me? What if someone sees us together?"

"Never mind that. Look." He stepped to one side.

In front of him the air shimmered like a heat-haze on a desert road. The ghostly smell of chips was at its peak here. It was like being haunted by a McDonald's. The shimmering effect was contained to a small, irregular outline just a few centimetres in diameter.

"Uh, what is that?" I said.

Stellar reached an investigative finger towards what I was rapidly coming to the conclusion must be a glitch in reality. "I think it's a –"

There was a blur of movement and something shot out of the hole with a squeak. I jumped back.

"– gerbil," finished Stellar.

The small creature skidded along the floor, its tiny claws skittering on the linoleum, and stopped at my feet. It had a tan and white coat and distinctive black marks over its eyes like a superhero mask.

"Wayne?" Stellar and I said at the same time.

We crouched down and studied what I now suspected to be my – *our* – former pet.

"I was just thinking about you," said Stellar to Wayne.

I'd been thinking about Wayne too, but I didn't imagine that'd make him suddenly jump out of a hole in the air. "It can't be Wayne. Can it?"

The gerbil lifted its tiny masked face to meet ours and for a moment I was convinced it could understand.

Then, to my astonishment, a pair of red beams shot from its eyes, blasted narrowly past my right ear and bored two tiny holes in the spine of a book on the shelf.

I could see Wayne adjust the angle of his head to line up another shot. If I didn't do something quickly I was about to get zapped by a gerbil with laser-eyes.

"Shoo!" I shouted. "Get off!"

Wayne ignored me.

In a flash Stellar directed his telekinetic power at the small creature, lifting it off the floor, sending it back through the hazy outline. It vanished; all that was left was a gerbil-shaped hole in the air. And then, with a long sucking noise, that was gone too.

"Impossible," Stellar muttered in the silence that followed. From his reaction I could tell that whatever just happened, it was new to him too.

"Luke?"

I swung round to see Lara standing in the aisle. She glared at me, tapping one foot.

"You need to have a word with yourself."

I glanced to my side. Stellar had vanished, though not in the same way as Wayne. At Lara's approach he'd swiftly concealed himself behind the nearest bookcase. I knew why he was avoiding her – because of the mission. Typical of the superheroes in our family, letting me deal with the irritating stuff.

"Did you hear me, Luke? You need to—"

"Is this about Stellar? I don't know why he won't have you on the mission. Have you talked to *him*?"

"I'm talking to you."

"We're not the same—" Oh, what was the point.

"I won't be left out. I'm a superhero like Star Lad, qualified to participate in all world-saving schemes. Why's he sidelined me, hmm? I'll tell you why – because I'm a girl."

"I don't think that's—"

She folded her arms. "This could go to court."

"What, the Superhero Employment Tribunal?"

"Are you making fun of me, Luke Parker?" She gave me no time to respond. "You're the leader of S.C.A.R.F. I want on that mission. Sort it."

"Yes, I… No problem. On it," I said. "I'm definitely on it."

With a withering look she turned on her heel and stormed off, only to pause at the end of the aisle. "Oh, one more thing. You also have to talk to Serge."

"About what?"

She squirmed. "You know."

I did not know.

"For goodness' sake," she said, fidgeting with her

sleeve. "His dislocation of undying love."

Oh. *That.* "I don't think he really meant it," I said, figuring it would be better for all concerned – but mainly me – just to smooth over the unfortunate incident. "He only said it because he thought it was the end of the world."

Lara frowned. "Is that what he told you?"

I ran through all the possible answers to that question and chose the one that I hoped would put a swift end to this conversation, even if it was not strictly true.

"Yes."

"Oh." She looked strangely hurt, but I had no idea why.

"Une gerbille?" remarked Serge with surprise.

"Not just any *gerbille*," I said. "Wayne the *gerbille*."

School was over for the day and Serge and I were heading to the comic shop to help with preparations for the grand reopening. On the way there I filled him in on the strange goings-on in the peculiarly dark library.

"We'd both been thinking about our old pet and then – *hey presto!* – he appeared. Well, not Wayne exactly. It was him, but he was more of an *enhanced* gerbil. The pet I always wished he'd be. Stellar seemed as surprised as I was."

"And you have tried to recreate the phenomenon, I presume?" said Serge.

What did he take me for? I'd been doing nothing else since it happened. All through double maths and PE I'd concentrated my mind on Wayne, picturing his chubby little body, hoping to summon him again. "Nothing," I said glumly. "Which means Stellar made him appear, not me."

"Ah *oui*, but appear from where?"

I'd been pondering that all afternoon and I had a theory. "In Stellar's universe he's me with powers, right? So what if in some alternate universe Wayne lived on and became the super-gerbil I always wanted?"

"In which case what you witnessed in the library was a wormhole," Serge concluded, "or per'aps more accurately, a *gerbille-*'ole in the fabric of the universe."

That made perfect sense. I could always rely on Serge for a pinpoint analysis of the strangest events.

"So Stellar has the ability to summon gerbils between universes," he mused. "I must say that for a superpower it is rather *niche*."

"What if it's not just gerbils?" I said. "There are superheroes in comics who can manipulate the fabric of space and time, create doors between universes, even create whole universes." Stellar's strange new power made me anxious. Flying, force fields, even telekinesis were all pretty straightforward. Opening holes in the universe smacked of meddling with things best left alone. We turned into the High Street. "I wonder what else he can bring into existence."

5
WHEN YOU WISH UPON
A STAR LAD

While Other Luke suffered through double maths and PE (we'd established that our timetables, like our noses and indeed the rest of our anatomy, were identical), I took the opportunity to return to IKEA. Wayne the gerbil's mysterious materialisation in the library had thrown up some questions, and I was counting on the ship's computer having the answers.

The store was quiet and it wasn't long before I had the interdimensional bedroom to myself. I sat down in the command sofa. Recognising my presence, the ship fired up its onboard systems.

"Running diagnostics," cooed the computer, which was

still masquerading as a KLABB bedside lamp with a light-brown textured shade. Everything was in good shape for my return journey with Zack in one week's time. In the meantime I was looking forward to hanging out in this world. Things were so much simpler here. Stupid Other Luke didn't appreciate how good he had it.

I noticed a few changes from the last time I was here. One wall of the bedroom set was covered in wallpaper that featured a pattern made up of illustrations of computers. The bed had acquired a computer-themed duvet cover and pillow set, and there was a series of black and white prints of famous computers on the opposite wall.

"I like what you've done with the place," I said.

The lamp-light turned from red to green, indicating a problem. "Fuel depleted," it announced.

This was bad news. "What does the ship run on?"

"K'Bhejup beans," it answered. "A synthetic plant-based fuel unique to the planet Trolox in the Caspian system."

This wasn't bad, it was catastrophic.

"So how am I supposed to refuel? It's not as if I can pop into Tesco and pick up a packet of what d'you call them? Ketchup beans?" A slim TV hung in the centre of one wall. The computer projected the alien name on to it and my tongue made an attempt to get round the strange word. "*K'Bhejup* beans."

No sooner had it passed my lips when the bedroom began to rock as if it was being buffeted by storm winds.

"Warning! Warning!" The computer blared. "Dimensional anomaly alert!"

Before me the air vibrated like the surface of a still pond broken by a dropped pebble. There was a sucking sound and at the centre of the pulsing waves formed a tiny black hole. What's more, I could smell chips. Exactly the same thing had happened in the school library.

"Danger! Danger!" shrieked the computer.

What could it be – another laser-gerbil? Or worse?

With a pop, something shot out of the hole. As it flew past my head I snapped it out of the air with my telekinesis. There on my palm lay a small purple bean.

"K'Bhejup bean," declared the computer.

No way! "Did you do that?"

"Negative."

A thought that had been forming since the events in the library now took shape. "Did *I* do it?"

Before the ship could answer, there was more popping, as if all the weasels in the nursery rhyme had gone off at once, and more beans flew out of the hole, quickly coating the floor. They continued to pour out, rising to a height that covered my ankles, before the stream turned to a trickle and finally dried up.

"Reviewing fuel status," said the computer. It paused to perform complex calculations, before adding, "There are enough K'Bhejup beans for a full tank."

I began scooping them up into one of those giant blue IKEA bags. But as I collected the precious fuel, a great creaking noise echoed through the store, like a thousand sleepers in a thousand KOPARDAL beds all turning over at once. The floor shook, shelves trembled sending ornaments crashing to the floor, and then with a sucking noise like someone wading through a muddy bog in wellies, the mysterious hole vanished.

"OK, computer, tell me what's going on." I picked up a handful of beans. "How did these get here?"

The lamplight flashed away as the super-intelligent computer blabbed on for ages, describing the science behind the creation of the holes. Here are the highlights of our conversation:

Computer: "Dimensional Rift Yada Yada Identical Twin completely Hawking unfathomable."

Me: "So what you're saying is that me and Other Luke were never meant to meet. And when two versions of the same person come together they generate a strange force between them. Not like the actual Force, more like a magnetic field, but weirder."

Computer: "Quantum-y Stargate Blah-Blah

Incomprehensible Space Thingy."

Me: "And thanks to my awesome powers I am able to super-charge this weird magnetic field, allowing me to pull objects – like a K'Bhejup bean or a laser-gerbil – from their universes into this one."

Computer: "Affirmative Superposition Probability Gerbil Amplitude Heisenber-ghastly."

Me: And whenever I do that I create one of those shimmering hole thingies. So they're portals to other universes. Fascinating. Do you want to go into detail about how those work?

Computer: No.

This was so brilliant. It was like I'd been granted three wishes, but instead of three I had a whole infinite multiverse of wishes. "I wonder what I'd like next," I mused. "Thor's hammer, or Captain America's shield, or—"

"Do you have this in red?" said a voice.

I looked up to see a man with black-rimmed glasses and a neatly trimmed beard holding the super-computer-disguised-as-a-bedside-lamp.

"Uh, I don't work here. Sorry."

"Oh. I see." He paused, and remained exactly where he stood. "Do you know if it comes in red?"

What was it with some people?! With one thought I could have summoned the Ultimate Nullifier and wiped him from existence, erasing even the memory of him from the minds of everyone he knew. Instead, I pointed to a shelf stacked with boxes at the edge of the room set. "Top row. And it also comes in something called *lapis*. Goes well with the OTTIL cushion."

As he headed off I wished all the problems in my world could be fixed by a surprisingly good-value cushion cover. I glanced at the SVÄRTA bunk bed and felt a pang. Zack used to have bunk beds and occasionally he'd let me sleep in his room (on the bottom bunk, obviously). I sighed. Little did the others know, but Gorgon the World-Eater was the least of my problems.

6
STAR DAD

"I've figured out Stellar's evil plan," I announced to Serge and Lara as we walked home from school.

"I didn't know he had one," said Lara.

Was she bonkers? "Of course he has one! Why else is he in our world?"

"Uh, to recruit Star Lad for an upcoming battle with a fearsome enemy. Y'know, like he said?"

"Yes, yes, yes, I know all that, but don't you think it's suspicious? The way he just showed up like that and suddenly he and Zack are like this." I crossed my fingers.

"Are you certain this is not the green-eyed monster speaking?" asked Serge.

"What – the Hulk?"

"*Non*, I refer to *envy*. Stellar is spending a lot of time with your brother."

It was true. For several days I'd been forced to watch as, at every opportunity, Stellar wheedled his way further into Zack's good books. Between mocks and supervillain strategy sessions I couldn't get five minutes alone with my brother, but somehow he had endless time for Stellar. As soon as Zack finished school, the two of them would gather in the tree house to plan their superpowered defence against Gorgon the World-Eater. And during these sessions I wasn't even allowed in my own tree house. Outrageous! They didn't want S.C.A.R.F.'s help at all, though they weren't shy about accepting an endless supply of Serge's home baking. In fact, there was only one person Zack would ditch Stellar for, and that was Cara.

We'd reached the bus stop. Lara was catching the 162 to her dad's new flat across town but we still had a few minutes before it arrived.

"So, do you want to hear my theory or not?" I asked.

She and Serge waited expectantly for my shocking revelation.

"Stellar is planning to replace *me*." It was so obvious, I kicked myself for not figuring it out sooner. "He wants to take over my life."

Lara frowned. "Uh, OK. But why?"

She may have been super-smart but sometimes she could be slow on the uptake. "Because that's what evil twins do. Right, Serge?"

Serge nodded. "It is standard operating procedure in situations like this. The bad twin takes on the life of the good twin, using his uncanny likeness to fool even his closest friends." He gasped and took a step back. "What if you have already been substituted?"

"That is a very good point," I said.

Lara threw up her hands. "No, it's not. It's ridiculous." She gave a long sigh. "Just to be clear. You're saying that Stellar wants to swap his awesome superhero life in his world to be a perfectly average schoolboy who'll be lucky to pass maths in this one?"

"Well, sure, when you put it like that…"

"Don't take this the wrong way, Luke, but what do you have that he could possibly want?"

"Loads of stuff."

"Such as?"

I racked my brains. From comic collections to mid-level exam results, the truth was that Stellar and I possessed all the same things. The only exception being the small matter of superpowers.

"And how does the *gerbille-*'ole in the library fit into his dastardly mission?" asked Serge.

Yeah, there *was* that. "OK, OK, so maybe I don't know how all the pieces of the jigsaw fit together yet. But I will. And when I do, don't blame me if it's a jigsaw of *horror*."

"Unless at that point you have already been replaced," added Serge.

"Well, yes. But barring that."

Lara's bus pulled up and we went our separate ways: she to her dad's place, Serge to his house for "Soufflé Night". I went home and a short time later I was in our kitchen with Mum, laying the table for dinner. Dad hadn't yet returned from the comic shop. As the launch day approached he was putting in increasingly long hours. He used to work with Mum at the insurance company, but they'd let him go or, as Lara put it, "made him recumbent". Which was surprisingly accurate for her, as he'd spent a large amount of time lying on the sofa. Those days were over. He bustled about the shop like a general, directing the builders, offering unwelcome advice to Sidney, Layla and Jared, the art school students painting the Star Lad superhero mural, and juggling bunnies for the Dark Flutter petting zoo. It was nice to see him so happy. In fact, I hadn't seen him this energised since I accidentally rewired the plug on his laptop.

There was the click of the front door and a few seconds later Dad strolled into the kitchen, holding up two red capes side by side.

"Right, I've made up my mind. I'm going as Superman. I just haven't decided whether it'll be Earth-Two Superman, or Red Son Superman."

He had decided to reopen the shop with a cosplay promotion; anyone who came on the day dressed as a superhero or supervillain would receive a discount off their first purchase and a limited-edition, numbered shard of the Nemesis asteroid that had almost wiped out Earth. (Dad had found a pile of rocks in the back room, which I figured Christopher Talbot had left behind after using them in his many superpower experiments.)

"What about you?" he asked Mum. "Any thoughts on Wonder Woman?"

She pulled a face. "They haven't yet built the control tights to get me into that outfit."

From the hallway came the sound of the front door again. A breathless Zack blew into the kitchen. He wasn't alone. Next to him stood Cara. Recently I'd observed her at close quarters, conducting her own one-girl insurgency aboard an alien mothership, disrupting the invaders' plans and generally bringing down large dollops of havoc on their heads. She was impressive – no wonder Zack was obsessed with her.

He fizzed like a lit firework. "We were supposed to be studying at Cara's house, but her mum double-booked her book club so we've come here instead. For the peace and quiet. And can Cara stay for dinner?"

Cara cast a puzzled look at Zack. "I thought we were just doing physics?"

"Of course, of course, but shall we not study better after our *repast?*" Zack said in this weird voice.

Mum and Dad exchanged looks.

"You're very welcome to stay, Cara," said Mum. "Tonight's *repast* is not quite *cordon bleu*, I'm afraid, just pizza and salad."

Zack put his fingers to his lips and made a kissing noise. "Ahh, the classic dish of the Neapolitans. *Bellissima.*"

"I thought it was from Iceland," I said.

Zack scuttled over to the table and slid out a chair. "Permit me."

"Uh, thanks," said Cara, lowering herself into the seat.

"If I'd had a girl, I'd have called her Cara," said Mum, offering her some pizza. "Such a beautiful name."

Cara's polite thank you was interrupted by Zack.

"You know, it's also the name of a *ravishingly* beautiful

island in the Inner Hebrides. And *cara mia* is Italian for 'my love'. There. More Italian." He gave this little laugh. "I may break out into an *aria*."

He had completely lost it. I would've said Cara was looking at him like he was an alien from another planet, but I'd seen her expression in that situation and it was different.

"Kara's also Supergirl's name," I chipped in, "except hers starts with a 'K', not a 'C'."

"I don't know much about superheroes, kid," she said. She always called me kid.

"But you actually met Star Lad," said Dad. "That day with the bus was quite something."

Dad didn't know about our adventures aboard the sue-dunham mothership. He was referring to the first time Cara met Star Lad, which was ages ago when he had caught her falling from a runaway bus. Saving the passengers was the first superheroic thing my brother ever did. The moment had been captured forever – there was a poster and everything.

"Y'know what's funny?" she said. "When he was holding me so close like that, I tried to sneak a look under his hoodie. I thought he seemed familiar." Her eyes flicked on to Zack's. "Have you heard the rumour?"

Uh-oh.

53

"What rumour?" said Mum.

"They're saying that Star Lad is a boy at our school. And not just any boy." Cara pointed a triangle of pizza at Zack.

There was a pause, and then Mum and Dad burst out laughing.

I could see Zack's mouth do this crazy movement. A momentary pout followed by a swift upturn as he fixed a grin to his face and joined in with the incredulous laughter.

"Zack? Zack is Star Lad?" Crumbs of pizza base spilled from Dad's mouth. "Luke, can you imagine? Your brother. A superhero."

"Yes, so funny," I mumbled, avoiding Zack's gaze. In a way it was a shame we couldn't let Dad in on his eldest son's secret. If anyone would appreciate being the father of a superhero, it was him. The problem was he'd be *too* appreciative. I had no doubt he'd immediately get a mug with *Star Dad* on it, and then show up at the next school parents' evening in a T-shirt with "Yes, My Son *is* Star Lad" printed on the front in big flashing letters.

Dad ruffled Zack's hair. "Oh, if only, son. D'you know how much it would be worth to have Star Lad at the comic-shop launch?"

Zack's fake grin fell from his face. "How much?"

He and I had already discussed the possibility of Star Lad making an appearance. I'd suggested we attach coloured smoke canisters to his ankles, like the Red Arrows, and he fly over the shop a few times. But Zack had rejected the idea.

"Think it through, Luke," he'd said. "Why would Star Lad show up to a random comic shop launch? It wouldn't take an evil genius to figure out there's a connection. Next thing you know, I'd be outed."

As much as Star Lad's presence would have boosted sales, I knew he was right.

There was one good thing about my parents' amused reaction to the suggestion that Zack was Star Lad: if Cara had suspected it to be true, then they had put her off the scent. From then on dinner passed in a succession of mooning glances and forced laughs, as Zack seemed to find everything that Cara said or did either downright charming or side-splittingly funny. He kept refilling her water glass and throwing back his head with a hysterical giggle. It was *weird*. As far as I could tell, all the girl did was eat more pepperoni pizza than her fair share, and half the salad. Zack's behaviour was extra irritating since I had important information to pass on, but he was too distracted to pay attention.

Dinner finally came to an end. Cara settled herself in

the living room for her physics tutoring session while I cornered Zack over a sink full of dirty dishes. We used to have a dishwasher, but it didn't survive Dad's attempts at making an automated plate-rack. Zack washed and I dried.

"Isn't Cara amazing?" he gushed.

Amazing at eating pizza, yes. As much as I admired Cara I wasn't in the mood to hear about her right now, so before he could start talking about her again I said, "I don't think Stellar is telling us everything."

Zack gave an offhand shrug. "A supervillain threatens his world and he needs my help. What else is there to tell?"

"Uh, a few more details might be nice, y'know, before you swan off with a complete stranger to *another universe*."

"He's hardly a stranger though, is he?"

"How many times do I have to say it – he's not me. I mean, maybe we were the same person for the first eleven years of our lives, but not since he became all superpowered."

Zack rinsed a knife and tossed it on the draining board. "You're just jealous."

"Of course I'm jealous! But that doesn't mean I'm wrong. Let's look at the facts. There isn't a single example in comics or films where a twin shows up who isn't *evil*."

Zack creased his brow. "You know that's not strictly speaking a fact, right?"

I counted off on my fingers. "He's evil. He has superpowers. Therefore he must be a supervillain. I don't know what you're finding so hard about this."

"Fair enough," Zack said, much to my surprise. "In the past I've dismissed you, only to find out at the last minute – sometimes quite literally – that you were right all along." He handed me a dripping dinner plate. "So, what's the deal with Stellar? Let me guess. Some kind of outrageous interdimensional bank heist? No, wait. It's something involving a highly unstable alien substance and a chain of undersea volcanoes? Or is it the classic take-over-the-world-with-bees scenario? So, what've you got?"

Bees? What had he been reading? What I had wasn't any of that stuff. It was more of a hunch. "He took on a laser-gerbil in the school library, which I think he summoned through a hole in the fabric of space."

"What a supervillain!" Zack made a mocking face. "A genuine Les Luthor."

Did my brother really think the criminal mastermind who plagued Superman was some bloke called *Les*? Sometimes I despaired. "What about the gerbil-hole?

You have to admit that's suspicious."

"All right, tell you what," Zack said, scraping cheese from the last plate. "Stellar and I are planning to leave Saturday, right after the launch of Dad's comic shop. You've got until then to bring me some actual dirt." He lowered his washing-up brush. "I should go. Cara is waiting for me." With that, he hurried out of the kitchen, humming one of Billy Dark's lesser-known and therefore cooler songs.

My mission was clear: before Dad drew the winner of the cosplay competition on Saturday afternoon, I had to produce a smoking gun. Well, not literally. There was no time to lose. I decided to confront Stellar right away.

7
TREMORS

I found Stellar in my room, sprawled on my bed reading an issue of *The Amazing Spider-Girl*, his cape fanned out behind him, rising and falling as if held up on currents of air. He looked up from behind the comic with a grin.

"Hey, Luke!"

I gawped at him. "Are you mad? What are you doing in here?" I heard my parents stroll past the door. "What if they see us together?"

"Sorry." He lowered his voice. "Hope you don't mind, but I fancied hanging out in my bedroom again. With all my old childhood things."

I was outraged at his cheek. "Old childhood things? Too grown up for all this stuff, are you? Got rid of everything in your world then?"

"Uh … no. Course not. It's just … spending a week in a tree house changes you. Also, it was kind of cold out there."

This wasn't how I'd hoped our encounter would go. He had wound me up again and now I was the one on the defensive. I attempted to get things back on track.

"I never said thanks for saving my life in the library. If it hadn't been for you I would've been zapped by a laser-gerbil. That would've made some epitaph."

"No problem. Did you happen to mention to Zack what I did?"

I nodded. Stellar seemed pleased to hear that Zack knew of his exploits.

"It's funny seeing him as a superhero," he said. "Back in my universe he left the tree house before Zorbon arrived. If he had stayed put, everything would have turned out differently."

"It did," I reminded him bitterly.

Strangely, Stellar didn't look as smug or triumphant as I expected. In fact, he seemed kind of sad. Not Spider-Man-watching-Green-Goblin-toss-his-girlfriend-from-a-bridge sad, but definitely gloomy. A second later, Stellar seemed to pull himself together and gave a short laugh.

"While we're on the subject, who calls himself *Star Lad*? What kind of a name is *that*?"

Uh, the kind I came up with.

"That whole -lad, -man, -boy thing is so last century. Right, Luke?"

"Right," I agreed. Star Lad *was* kind of old-fashioned. On the other hand, Stellar was cutting-edge superhero nomenclature. Why hadn't I thought of it? I had to admit that he was good at being a superhero. Not that I should've been surprised. He was, after all, me. Given the unique situation, I had to ask the question that had obsessed me since I cracked open my first comic.

"What does it feel like to have powers?" I asked. "Zack's tried to explain, but we're talking about someone who thinks Superman's weakness is Samsonite."

I could see him contemplate his answer. "It's great," he said at last.

"That's not an answer. I want details, insight. *Texture*. Maybe you've forgotten what it used to be like. Being me. I'm stuck like this all the time. I can't quick-change into a cool costume and go off and save the world. But you can. At three fifteen every weekday I walk home from school. If you wanted, you could fly home … via the Alps! Not me. Everyone tells me what to do, all the time. Mum, Dad, teachers. I have no power. I'm not even allowed to choose my own wallpaper. But you – you can do *whatever* you like." I finished my rant slightly breathless.

"You're right," he said. "I wouldn't change it. For the world."

It was weird. Even though he was talking about the most exciting thing that could possibly happen to a person, he sounded unenthusiastic.

"I'd give anything—" I began.

He cut me off. "No. You wouldn't." His mouth turned down. "Having superpowers is awful. A burden I wouldn't wish upon my worst enemy."

I studied his unhappy face. He sounded oddly convincing. Maybe really good acting was one of his superpowers. "You're saying that just to make me feel better, aren't you?"

He grinned. "Absolutely."

Gah! I knew it. I knew having superpowers would be the best thing ever. It wasn't fair! Why did it have to happen to *him me*, instead of *me me*?

"I know what you're thinking." He put down the comic and got to his feet. We stood there, the before and after frames in a superhero transformation sequence.

"Let's not kid around any more. You believe I'm your Evil Twin. That I'm Carnage to your Spider-Man, Abomination to your Hulk."

"Killer Moth to my Batman," I added for good measure.

Stellar nodded his head appreciatively. "Nice one. Mothcave, Mothmobile, not forgetting the Moth-Signal." He stroked his cape thoughtfully. "Your suspicion is perfectly natural. In your place, I'd be thinking the same. So, we need to establish beyond doubt that I'm a good guy. You should interrogate me." He grabbed my Human Torch bedside lamp and, shining it into his own face, said, "Ask me anything."

"Won't your parents have noticed that you're missing?"

"They think I'm on a school trip," said Stellar. "Right now they believe I'm building confidence and self-esteem at a multi-activity residential adventure centre in Devon."

"The one with the heated pool and the ski slope?" My school in my universe had organised the identical trip. "My parents wouldn't let me go. They need every penny right now for the new shop."

"That sucks," said Stellar. "Our parents can be real killjoys, right? Have you noticed that every time we ask for something cool for our birthday, they always give us –"

"– shoes," we said at the same time. I looked at him and we both burst out laughing.

"And it's not like they're rocket shoes or anything good like that," he added.

"Rocket shoes would be cool," I agreed. Then I stopped myself. This was a serious interrogation. "You say you need Zack to help save your world, but crossing dimensions isn't like taking the bus to the High Street. How do you plan to travel back with him to your universe?"

"Zorbon the Decider is picking us up," Stellar answered smartly. "You know Zorbon, right?"

"We haven't met." I failed to keep the resentment from my voice. "We keep missing each other."

"Oh, Zorbon's great. You'd really like him." He grinned. "You *do*."

So far my interrogation had failed to dent Stellar's irritatingly cheery armour. It was time for a different approach.

"In the school library, it was you who made Wayne appear, wasn't it?"

He paused. His expression told me he was weighing up whether or not to tell me the truth.

"It was me, yeah."

I pounced on his admission. "I knew it! But what I don't get is why Zorbon would give you a power like that?"

"He didn't. It turns out that comics were right after all. When two versions of the same person meet it *is* like matter and antimatter. Except not as dangerous. Seems that when we're together you and I create a weird magnetic field. I'm north to your south, positive to your negative."

Evil to my good, I thought to myself.

"We have a magnetic personality," he beamed and then closed his eyes. His brow furrowed in concentration.

I wrinkled my nose at a familiar smell. "*Chips.* Stellar, no. Not here!"

It was too late. In the corner of the room the air rippled and formed a new hole, although the outline of this one was definitely not that of a gerbil. It looked like a foot.

Stellar's eyes blinked open and something shot out of the hole. It flew around the room, bouncing off the ceiling and walls like a pinball. I saw with alarm that it was heading straight at me. There was no time to duck. It loomed large in my vision, and then, mere centimetres away from smacking into my face, it split in two. I felt my hair part as each half flew by one side of my head.

It was a pair of somethings.

"Rocket shoes!" I goggled at the incredible sight. A pair of ordinary black leather school shoes, with the unlikely addition of rocket engines in the heels. They hovered over my bed.

Stellar's eyes were wide with wonder. "D'you see what I did?"

Before I could reply, the floor began to tremble and a vibration shook the house. From outside tree branches creaked and popped like a submarine's hull at depth. The Human Torch lamp slid across the bedside table, crashed to the floor, flickered and went out. A second later there was a click of circuit breakers as the house lost power and all the lights failed. In the dark I stumbled and lost my footing, twisting my ankle as I fell. I rolled under my bed, sheltering there for cover. There was a roar as the rocket shoes ignited once again, followed by a crash and a terrible ripping noise. The tremor subsided and the world steadied itself once more. Light spilled through the house as the power flicked back on.

I realised I couldn't hear the rockets and it was safe to poke my head out from beneath the bed. The gerbil-hole had vanished, but I saw with a sinking heart that it had been replaced by another hole. The rocket shoes had blasted clean through my bedroom ceiling and the roof.

Beyond a ragged opening of plaster and broken tiles lay the night sky.

From outside my door came the sound of scuffling feet. Stellar didn't hang around. He shot out of the hole in the ceiling seconds before Mum and Dad burst into my room, quickly followed by Zack and Cara. Once they'd established that I was in one piece their attention turned to the less-than-one-piece ceiling. I couldn't tell them what had happened, but they didn't ask, instead putting the damage down to the freak earthquake, which was half true.

"Well, you won't be sleeping in here for a while," said Dad.

Mum agreed. "You'll have to move in with Zack while the roof's repaired."

"No way!" Zack complained. "He can't—"

Mum cut him off with a look. It was like General Zod's just after deciding to destroy Earth, except more dangerous. "Cara, I think you'd better go home now," she said. "I need Zack to help move furniture."

I looked up into Zack's glowering face. Not only was I about to become his unwelcome guest, I had also brought his cosy tutoring session with Cara to an untimely end. Stellar had really dropped me in it.

I hadn't found out much, but I was more convinced

than ever that Stellar was hiding a dark secret. Something about him wasn't right. One moment he was his usual swaggering, smug self, who wouldn't shut up, and the next he was quiet and sad. My super-twin was super-moody.

8
TWINKLE, TWINKLE, LITTLE DEATH STAR

Dad attempted a makeshift repair, nailing a piece of plastic sheeting (and his tie) across the hole in the roof. We spent the remainder of the evening moving stuff out of my room, in case it rained. I tried to tell my furious brother that it wasn't my fault, but he'd made up his mind. I was in the dog-house.

I brushed my teeth and fumed. Stellar was reckless. Dangerous. I planned to give him a piece of my mind, but I'd have to wait until everyone else was in bed. I headed to Zack's room. In our old house Zack would occasionally let me sleep in his bunk bed (on the bottom, obviously). I missed those days. Under less shout-y circumstances I would've been looking forward to our sleepover.

I was in bed before Zack. On his side of the room a white lamp glowed from a bedside table. His duvet was a simple blue stripe; not a single Jedi or superhero decorated it. Zack didn't see the point of any of that stuff. I remembered years ago, when Dad bought him a Spider-Man pillow set. He'd shoved it to the back of the wardrobe, crammed under a pile of shoes, where it had lain for months. Even at that age (I was four), I sensed that his lack of appreciation for the finer things in life – i.e. comic-books and lightsabers – was weird. It wasn't as if he preferred opera and ate olives, but at seven years old he seemed different from anyone else.

It would remain like that for years. Growing up I always had friends over to play. Zack played host to the occasional schoolmate, but they never came more than once. He was serious, and always seemed to be worried about something. It's hard to explain, but he didn't appear worried for himself. He was like a lighthouse, standing at the edge of the world, anxious that everyone else got home safely.

Once I overheard Mum and Dad talking about him. Long after bedtime I'd left Zack asleep in our room to creep downstairs. I recall being on a mission to adjust the boiler settings. From an early age I displayed an uncontrollable urge to randomly push buttons and turn dials on any control panel within my short reach – an instinct that has since served me well in my adventures with supervillains and alien overlords. But which probably means I shouldn't consider a career as a nuclear missile operator. As I sneaked past the kitchen door I heard Mum and Dad talking inside.

"Zack'll be fine," said Dad. "I was twice as weird when I was a kid and look how great I turned out."

There was a long pause before Mum spoke. "He's different – special. Luke is too, of course. But not like Zack. There's something about that boy…"

I felt a pain in my chest. Not like the time I'd gulped down half a bottle of Dad's chilli sauce on a dare. This was more of a dull ache. Standing on the other side of the door, I knew this was a conversation I shouldn't be eavesdropping on, but I couldn't walk away.

"Hey, maybe that's it," said Dad. "Zack's name is on some ancient mystical scroll and he's foretold in prophecy to save the world. See, the weight of his destiny is why no kid will play with him."

"Are you going to take this seriously?"

They carried on their discussion, but I'd stopped listening. All I knew was that Zack was the most important person in my life. My world revolved around him. He was the sun and I was Mercury, which at a distance of 57 million kilometres is the closest planet in our solar system to the sun. He was my best friend. He was a total pain. He was my big brother.

Zack swept into the room. "You'd better not snore," he said, climbing into bed. He snapped off the light, pulled his covers up and turned his back on me.

I wanted to discuss Stellar's suspicious new power; ask him what he thought about the holes in the fabric of the universe. I wanted my brother's advice.

I sat up. "Do you remember my gerbil, Wayne?"

There was a groan from beneath Zack's duvet. "Go to sleep."

Perhaps jumping straight in with questions about weird dimensional pets was the wrong approach. I needed to ease him into the conversation. When I thought of our old bedroom I also pictured Mum or Dad, sitting uncomfortably on an understuffed beanbag reading us bedtime stories. "What about Dad's nursery rhymes? They were great. Remember 'Twinkle, Twinkle, Little Death Star'?" In Dad's versions of nursery rhymes, boring old kings and queens became all-powerful galactic emperors, black sheep transformed into black ops, and the three blind mice were ninja masters. And let's not even start with the mutant creatures lurking on Old Macdonald's farm.

I began to recite.

"Twinkle, twinkle, little Death Star,
How I wonder at your firepower,
Up above my homeworld so high,
Raining fiery terror from the sky."

"He only did those for you," Zack muttered.

I detected a note of hurt in my brother's voice. "That's because he knew you weren't into any of that stuff," I said. "You wouldn't get the references."

"The two of you did loads of things like that," he grumbled. "You and Dad went to that comic convention in Birmingham, you built the Lego Death Star without me and you spent ages making those Top Trump superhero cards together."

The convention had been brilliant fun, I remembered constructing the Death Star and fixing its little thermal exhaust port flaw, but I hadn't thought about those cards in years. One wet afternoon we'd sat at the kitchen table and invented a whole world of goodies and baddies, each with a detailed list of his or her own strengths, weaknesses and, of course, superpowers. I gave them badly spelled names and drew them on individual cards. What had I called it? "Hearos & Vilanz," I said, remembering.

"That was it. And when I said I wanted to play, you wouldn't let me," said Zack. "You threw a total fit. It was the same with that Spider-Man pillow set Dad bought me. You took one look at it and started crying that you wanted it. In the end, I hid it in the wardrobe, just to stop your whining."

I didn't remember it like that, but having got it off his chest, Zack rolled over and settled down for the night. I waited until I was sure he was asleep, then crept out of bed and made my way through the silent house to the garden.

The tree house lay before me, silhouetted against the blue-black sky. It had been completely rebuilt after what my parents believed was an accidental fire caused by a faulty novelty Thor lamp, but was in fact due to a booby-trapped alien TV remote control. Dad had since installed a smoke alarm that was so sensitive it went off if you so much as mouthed the word "smoke". A pinprick of light shining from inside told me that Stellar had ignored my instruction not to draw attention to his presence. I hadn't wanted to let him stay here at all but the others overruled me. It was my Batcave, my Fortress of Solitude, my Rebel base. And there was a superpowered cuckoo in my nest.

"Did you see that?" Stellar shouted delightedly as I

stormed in. "I thought about rocket shoes and – *whammo!* – the universe sent me a pair."

"You're crazy, y'know that. You wrecked my room. And I'm pretty sure your power caused that earthquake."

"I'd hardly call it an earthquake. At most it was a tremor."

That was not reassuring. "This superpower of yours – are you sure it's *safe*?"

"Hey, you can't make an interdimensional omelette without breaking a few supermassive eggs."

I had a strong suspicion that he was playing down the bad side. Punching holes in the universe sounded like the sort of thing that came with dire consequences. So far he had outmanoeuvred me like an X-Wing dogfighting with a Sopwith Camel, but I was determined to end the day one step ahead of my twin.

"We didn't finish the interrogation," I said.

He opened his arms wide. "Shoot."

"Why don't you want Lara to come with you to your world?"

He looked down at his feet then back at me. "Her superpower, it's, well … a bit rubbish."

To be fair, I used to think the same thing. Clearly, in his universe he hadn't seen her in action against alien invaders.

"She has skunk hair," I said.

"Really? Now, that is cool."

I explained how Lara had used her power to save my neck against the Alien Overlord.

"Y'know what," he said when I'd finished, "you've convinced me. Dark Flutter ought to be on the mission. The more superheroes the better, right?"

I hadn't expected him to agree so readily. I felt wrong-footed again by my equal and opposite number. At least Lara would be pleased.

It was getting late. "I have to go," I said. At the door I stopped and looked back. Stellar hadn't moved. It's the strangest feeling to be watched so intently through your own eyes. He knew exactly how I thought, what I knew, and how I'd react in any given situation. I searched his face for a clue to his real plan. Either he was telling the truth and everything would be fine, or I was facing the deadliest enemy I'd yet encountered.

Me. With superpowers.

9
ENDLER'S GAME

In science an event horizon is the point of no return, the place in the universe from which nothing escapes. Or, as I preferred to call it, double maths with Mrs Endless. (Her real name is Endler, but honestly, who could resist?) As she droned on about integers I glanced up at the wall clock. The lesson still had fourteen hours left to go. Time stretched out like Mr Fantastic's arms. I yawned.

"Luke Parker." Mrs Endless's voice interrupted my comic-book daydream.

"Minus forty-two," I blurted out.

"Correct," she said, spectacles slipping down her nose.

Well, that was a piece of luck. "It is?"

"No," she snipped. "Not even close." She prodded her spectacles back up her nose. "Miss out on our beauty sleep last night, did we, Mr Parker?"

"No, Mrs Endless— *Endler!*" I offered up an apologetic little smile.

She glowered at me. "I had your brother in my class last year," Mrs Endless went on. (And on.) "Now, there's a boy who applied himself."

Here we go again, I thought. Another sharp reminder that Zack soared through his school career while I stumbled along behind him. I sighed inwardly.

"But then he does have the advantage of being *superpowered.*" There was a pause, and then Mrs Endless gave a great honking laugh, which while unsettling at least proved she didn't believe the rumour.

With Mrs Endless's seeming approval of the subject, the rest of the class began to discuss it in earnest. Conversations burst out like popcorn in a hot pan.

Josh Khan leaned over and whispered, "It's true, isn't it?"

I had to tread carefully. Josh already knew too much. "You've met Zack – does he strike you as the superhero type?" I said, trying to brush off his question while appearing unconcerned. Serge had informed me that in

French it's called being *blasé*.

Josh wasn't buying it, in any language. "You know Dark Flutter. It's hardly a stretch to imagine you also know her sidekick, Star Lad."

Sidekick? Uh, what version had he been watching?

I could almost hear his mind whirring as he laid out his thinking. "I bet he's a member of your secret squirrel gang. And that would explain why *you're* a member too. You've got no powers, you're useless at, well, pretty much everything. Your *brother* must have got you in."

There was never a pool full of piranhas around when you needed one.

"Right, that's quite enough chatter about Star Lad," said Mrs Endless, clapping for silence. "Now, class, let's have some fun *dividing* integers."

Sometime around the year 3000 double maths eventually came to an end. By comparison, the rest of the day passed in a blur, mostly because I had to move fast to stay one step ahead of Josh Khan. I daren't risk fielding any more of his questions, at least not until I'd filled Zack in. One wrong word could blow Star Lad's identity wide open.

I was just about to leave when I saw Josh hurrying towards me. To my surprise, he didn't stop to harass me with yet another irritating theory about my brother.

Instead, he raced past, shouting, "Star Lad's trying out for the running team!"

I hurried after him. *What* was going on now?

I arrived at the track and pushed my way to the front of the big crowd, just in time to see the climax of the latest heat. Out in front was Cara Lee. With a burst of speed around the final bend, she opened up a commanding lead on the rest of the pack. Arms pumping, knees rising to her ears, it seemed that her shoes barely touched the ground. She glided across the line, to victory.

I spotted Zack beside the track and made my way over. His eyes were latched on to Cara.

"What are you doing here?" I asked.

He tore his gaze away. "What does it look like? I'm trying out for the team."

"Uh, why? I mean, how have you got time for this? You have even less free time than me, and I had to give up Lego club to take care of my S.C.A.R.F. responsibilities."

He gave a sigh. "Why are you here, Luke?"

I ignored his unwelcome tone. "We have to talk. Josh Khan is on to us," I said. "And when I say us, I mean you."

He didn't seem to hear me. He was too focused on Cara ambling back across the track chatting to another runner, a girl called Izzy. She had curly blonde hair, so everyone called her Frizzy Izzy.

"Great race, Cara," beamed Zack. "You have lovely form." He shook out his arms and did a star-jumpy thing.

The two girls exchanged looks.

"Some crowd, huh?" Zack knelt to retie his shoelaces.

Cara glanced at the mass of spectators. "Mm-hmm," she agreed.

"Aren't there usually this many people?" he asked.

"Nope," said Cara. "I've never even seen this many people turn out for an actual competition. The only school spirit in this place is haunting the peculiarly dark library."

"So why are they all here?" asked Zack.

She gave him a look, as if to say, "Really, you have to ask?"

Just then the PE teacher blew his whistle.

"OK, flyboy, your turn," said Cara. "Into the blocks. And good luck."

"Yeah," said Frizzy Izzy with a teasing smile, "Good luck, *Star Lad*."

Zack's cheeks flushed scarlet and he turned to take in the cheering crowd. Finally it dawned on him why all these kids had stayed after school for a boring track meet. They'd shown up to see their very own superhero in action. Someone unfurled a long banner. Scrawled across it was the phrase, "Go, Star Lad! Go!"

I caught the grim expression on his face. He was hating this. The last time I'd seen him so uncomfortable was when Mum accidentally shrunk his favourite underpants and he'd insisted on wearing them.

Someone was waving at me from the edge of the whooping crowd. It was Lara. I left Zack to take his place with the rest of the runners and jogged over. I don't normally like to break into a run of any kind so I can only assume being around the athletics team must have brought it on.

"How did you know I was here?" I asked. Fair to say, the track was not my natural habitat.

"The school guinea pig saw you heading this way," she explained. She gave a nod in Zack's direction. "So, this must be his latest attempt to impress her."

"Impress who?"

Lara sighed. "My sister."

So that's what he was doing here. "Are girls impressed by boys who can run fast?" I asked.

"Yes, they can't help themselves. It's elocution."

What had speaking nicely got to do with it? I shook my head, mystified.

She huffed. "Y'know, Darwin's Theory of Elocution?

Fish turning into monkeys turning into people. For a cave-woman it was an attractive quality in a cave-man, being able to sprint after a woolly mammoth."

"I didn't think mammoths were that fast."

"Once they got going." She grabbed my sleeve. "But that's not why I came. I have something to tell you," she added cryptically, leading me out of earshot of the crowd.

"Me too," I said. "I have good news."

"And I have bad news."

We both hesitated.

"You should go first," she said. "You're not going to be very happy once you hear my news."

With a cry of "On your marks, set, go," the substitute teacher started the boys' race. Zack made a false start and the runners were called back to their blocks. As they settled for the restart, I filled Lara in on my conversation with Stellar.

"Stellar's changed his mind. You're on the team for the mission to the alternate universe. I told him about your skunk hair and—"

"Luke! You promised never to mention that again. It's so embarrassing! But y'know what, that doesn't matter now." She looked over her shoulder, double-checking to make sure we couldn't be overheard. "The rumour about your brother – something about it bothered me.

So I've been doing some digging."

In our last school Lara had been the youngest editor of the school newspaper. She used to say that she was not so much an eleven-year-old schoolgirl, more an investigative reporter embedded with Class 6b. She lowered her voice to a whisper. "The only people who know Zack's secret superhero identity are: Zorbon, obviously, since he gave him his powers; the members of S.C.A.R.F.; Christopher Talbot, last seen aboard an alien mothership shortly before it blinked out of existence—"

Once again Zack leapt from the start-line too soon – the Star Lad rumour had really got to him. The substitute gym teacher gave him a final warning. One more false start and he'd be out of the race.

"You think Christopher Talbot is the leak?" I had my doubts. "Even if somehow he is alive, spreading a mean rumour at a secondary school would be fairly low-level villainy, for him."

Lara gave an exasperated sigh. "I didn't say I believed it was him. Let me finish. I figured if I could find out where the rumour began then that would lead me to the original leak. So I asked around. Turns out the Quinn twins heard it from Daniel Garstang, who heard it from Talia Gardener, who heard it from Fairuzah Bashir, who heard it from Fee McKinnon, who heard it from ... *you*."

"Me? That's ridiculous. Of course it wasn't— Oh." It hit me. Now I knew who had started the rumour. The other day in the library I'd wondered why Stellar had been wearing my spare uniform. Now I knew.

"Exactly," said Lara. "The question is, why?"

"Because he's my Evil Twin."

"That's not really an answer, Luke."

I thought it was a perfectly good answer to a variety of questions, but it seemed I was the only one.

Lara sucked her top lip, which she did when she was deep in thought. Or eating peanut butter. "We need to ask ourselves, what does Stellar have to gain from giving away Zack's secret identity? What's his end-game?"

The substitute teacher fiddled with his stopwatch and restarted the boys' race. "On your marks. Get set... G ... ood grief!" He looked up in amazement. Like the rest of the crowd he was staring open-mouthed at the masked figure that had just swooped out of the bright-blue sky, cape streaming from his shoulders.

It was Stellar.

What was it with my double – didn't he understand the concept of keeping a low profile?

He shot over the heads of the runners preparing to race, and then, angling his body into the bends, streaked round the track. As he roared past the gawping crowd, he split the air with a sonic boom that blew the banner out of their hands. It flew up, carried on the current caused by his passing, before fluttering back down to earth, draping Zack and the rest of the runners.

"Star Lad! Whoo! Yeah!" whooped the crowd.

Star Lad – what were they on about? All eyes were focused not on Zack, but on Stellar. If he had stopped to sign autographs then the crowd would certainly have noticed the difference. But dressed in a similar costume, flying at speed, the two superheroes were indistinguishable.

Zack peeled off the banner and grinned.

"No one's going to believe he's Star Lad now," I mumbled. Stellar had pulled off a brilliant ruse.

"But it doesn't make any sense," said Lara. "Why would he spread the rumour, only to spelunk it?"

I was pretty sure she meant "debunk it", but I didn't bother correcting her. I watched Stellar soar into the distance. Once again he'd flown rings round all of us. What was he up to? Before the day was out, I swore I'd finally uncover the truth.

10
THE WONTON SOUP
REVELATION

"I owe you, big time," said Zack, gripping Stellar by the shoulders and beaming at him. It was later that evening and the three of us had gathered in the tree house for a debrief. As predicted, the crowd at the track believed they'd witnessed Star Lad breaking the lap record. Since Zack had at the time been standing on the start-line for all to see, as far as the kids in school were concerned that ruled him out as a potential candidate for the superhero's alter ego. The rumour was as dead as a doornail that my dad has attempted to hammer, which is very dead.

"I'm just glad I could help you," said Stellar.

The way he said it sounded so sincere. He had this

Evil Twin act down to perfection. First he'd started the rumour, then he'd put an end to it. Yet, as far as I could tell, the only thing he'd gained was Zack's gratitude. And how! My brother's opinion of him had shot up. Stellar was the best thing since rocket shoes.

"The nanosecond after the comic-shop launch tomorrow," said Zack, who'd sat his last mock that morning and seemed lost without them, "you and I are teaming up. Gorgon the World-Eater won't know what's hit him!"

I wanted to tell Zack about Stellar starting the very rumour he'd scotched, to warn him that Stellar was up to something. But we were in the dark about Stellar's plans. If my Evil Twin thought that we were on to him, we'd be giving up our only advantage.

Though, if I'm honest, I was also desperate to burst their brotherly bubble. All that was missing from their mutual appreciation society were matching T-shirts and an annual picnic. Stellar was getting on much better with Zack than I had for quite some time, and I didn't like it one bit.

"OK, I need your advice," began Zack.

This was a turn-up for the books. Zack rarely sought my opinion about anything these days, unless it was comic-book related, and then only grudgingly. "Ask away," I said.

"Not *your* advice." He turned to Stellar. "Did you see Cara Lee at the track?"

Stellar nodded. "I saw everyone thanks to my incredible Stellar Scanner."

He was such a bighead.

Zack began to pace. "It's quite clear to me that she's not interested in plain, ordinary Zack Parker." He stopped. "So I was wondering, what if I told her I was Star Lad?"

"You can't!" I blurted.

Zack shot me a dark look. "I didn't ask you." His eyes flicked across the room. "Stellar?"

"Other Luke is right," said Stellar reluctantly. At least my Evil Twin understood the rules about keeping your superhero identity under wraps.

Zack huffed. "Remind me again why not? I mean, honestly, what's the point of having a cool superhero secret if you can't use it to impress girls?"

"It's for her own good," said Stellar. "In comics the girlfriends of superheroes usually end up getting bumped off."

"You should listen to him," I said. "And anyway, who's to say Cara would even like you as Star Lad? Remember what happened aboard the sue-dunham mothership. The last time she relied on Star Lad to save her, she ended up having to save herself. I wouldn't count on her being *that* impressed."

"It's not fair!" he complained. "It's never going to happen between us."

"In my world," Stellar began, "you and Cara…"

Zack leapt on the unfinished statement. "Are we … together?"

He paused. "Sort of."

"What does that mean?" said Zack.

"That anything is possible." Stellar clicked his fingers. "I have a great idea. Why not use your telepathic power to probe Cara's mind and find out how she really feels about you?"

Zack squirmed. "I don't like to probe, not unless it's an emergency. And preferably never with someone I know. You have no idea the weird stuff people are thinking until you go swimming in their heads." He shivered. "Anyway, it contravenes Data Protection." He made his way to the door. "We should get going. Mum and Dad'll be waiting. Come on, Luke."

Stellar and I both went to follow him out.

Zack laughed. "Sorry," he addressed Stellar. "I meant the other Luke."

Now *I* was the *other* one – even to my own brother. Could this get any worse?

Zack exited the tree house and I could hear him chuckling at his mistake as he descended the rope ladder.

"I'm not so picky," said Stellar. He stood at the back of the tree house, half his face in shadow.

"About what?" I asked.

"Whose mind I probe." I glimpsed the flicker of a dark smile. "Minds are like messy drawers. You know what it's like, sometimes you need a double-A battery and you're sure there's one in there, but it's right at the back behind a ball of string and a used roll of Sellotape and if you're going to put your hands on it, then..." He stepped into the light. "You need to have a good rummage."

He studied me in silence. The only sound was the tap-tapping of bare branches against the tree house.

"Was that meant to be a threat?" I said. "Because, for future reference, no one ever sounded intimidating using the word 'rummage'. Got it?"

"I know you know," he said coolly. "You can't keep anything from me."

He'd crossed the line. I shook a warning finger. "Stay out of my mind, Stellar."

"I don't need to probe your mind, Luke." He lowered his voice to a growl. "I'm already in it. All. The. Time."

OK, now that was creepy. Just as I was mentally

measuring the distance to the door, Stellar gave a snort of amusement.

"You should see your face," he said, shoulders heaving with laughter. "Oh my goodness. That was brilliant. Did you like my Evil Twin act? *I'm already in it.* I thought the growly voice was a nice touch. What d'you think?"

I didn't know what to think. Which was the real Stellar – the exasperating prankster or the evil mastermind? He'd discombobulated me, again.

Shrugging off his villain act like it was a duffel coat, he crossed to the doorway and looked out over the garden towards the house. "What's for dinner?"

I could see Dad in the kitchen, criss-crossing frantically from one side to the other. Even from here I could tell that he was looking for his car keys.

"And please don't tell me I'm getting leftovers again," Stellar went on. "I'm hungrier than Gordon the World-Eater."

"We're going out for Chinese," I said.

He rubbed his hands together. "Great. Bring me back –"

"– wonton soup and a portion of sweet and sour chicken," we both said at the same time. Some superheroes were connected by telepathy. We were linked by Chinese food.

Hold on a minute. Rewind.

Did he just say *Gordon* the World-Eater?

The name echoed along the dustiest corridors of my mind, banging doors unopened for years. I'd heard it before, a long time ago, but until that moment it had been buried beneath the accumulated names of a thousand comic-book characters. Now it surfaced like a zombie hand reaching through the soil to clasp its fingers around my ankle.

"You OK?" asked Stellar. "You look like you just saw a ghost."

Not a ghost. A doppelganger. (Which is like an evil twin in fairy tales.) "Fine. I'm totally fine," I said, trying to keep my breath even, hoping he wouldn't see through me and realise his mistake. "Looks like Dad found his keys. I'll see you later."

"Don't forget the prawn crackers."

I scrambled down the rope ladder and dashed into the house, not daring to look back in case Stellar should glimpse my face and guess I was on to him.

"Luke, we're leaving, get in the car," said Dad as I shot past him and Mum at the foot of the stairs.

"I have to go to the toilet," I called back, and heard him mutter his frustration.

"Is it just me," he grumbled to Mum, "or is that boy

always going for a wee at the worst moment?"

"We'll be in the car!" Mum shouted after me.

It was a special night. We were all going out for dinner to celebrate the opening of the new comic shop, but The Mandarin would have to wait. The Chinese restaurant, that is, not the Marvel supervillain.

When I reached the landing I ignored the bathroom and dragged a chair beneath the attic hatch. I jumped up to grab the handle. The hatch swung open and I lowered the ladder from inside, quickly climbing up into the low-ceilinged room beyond. I snapped on an overhead light. A bare light bulb chased away the shadows around a cluster of plastic storage boxes. Most of them were helpfully labelled and contained things like old photo albums, Christmas decorations, baby clothes of mine and Zack's that Mum and Dad had inexplicably chosen to keep. I continued searching until I found a box with my name scrawled on it in Dad's handwriting. I prised off the lid. Inside was a collection of useless stuff: a lifetime of birthday cards; endless drawings I'd done over the years; a stack of finger-pointing school-report cards. Half hidden beneath a drawing I'd made at nursery school portraying me and my family – which at the time appeared to include robot supervillain Ultron – I found what I'd come for.

"Hearos & Vilanz," I muttered, lifting out the deck of homemade cards that Dad and I had created. Like a mini Zorbon the Decider I'd sat at the kitchen table and bestowed each character with superpowers. I riffled through the pack, skimming past Thunder-Shooter and Sky-Rabbit, Wonder-Gluk and Punch-Man. But it was none of these I was looking for.

Somewhere in the pack was the ultimate power. Strength: 100. Psionic ability: 100. Speed: 100. He was a hundred per cent across the board. All-powerful, invulnerable, indestructible. Even back then I'd read enough comics to know that any self-respecting fictional universe needed an invincible supervillain.

I found it! My fingers closed around the yellowing card as I read.

"Gordon the World-Eater."

The corners of the card were bent, and along the bottom edge ran a tear in my unbeatable villain. The drawing was surprisingly good. I'd given his body the classic overly muscled look, but instead of a masked or hooded face I'd made his head a black hole speckled with glitter to represent the worlds he'd eaten. Unlike the rest of the drawing where the felt tip pen had strayed over the lines, his head was perfect, as if the dark force at its centre had sucked the ink into a seamless circle. As I peered at it in the dim attic light, I felt a shiver.

"Gordon. *Gorgon*." It was too much of a coincidence. They had to be one and the same. "He's not real," I mumbled to myself. "There is no Gorgon the World-Eater." I pictured Stellar and me, each sitting down with our dad on that same wet afternoon all those years ago, separated only by a universe.

So how could Stellar's world be threatened by a made-up supervillain? The answer was that it couldn't. Which meant that Stellar had invented a fake threat to persuade Zack to go with him. But why? The answer struck me like a blow from Thor's hammer.

It was a trap for Star Lad.

I had to show the Top Trump card to Zack – he'd have to believe me now. I held up the precious card, and a shadow fell across it. I spun round. Stellar hovered above the attic hatch.

"You got me," he said. "*Gordon* the World-Eater." He shook his head. "I knew I'd slipped up as soon as I opened my mouth."

"I know what you're up to," I said

He smiled thinly. "You have no idea."

He pointed, and I could only watch in dismay as the Top Trump card wriggled free from my fingers and spun through the air into his outstretched palm. The one piece of evidence that proved Stellar's guilt was now in his possession.

Slowly my Evil Twin extended a hand. "Join me, Luke, and together we will rule the multiverse!" Then he snorted. "Just kidding."

11
THE QUANTUM TOILET QUANDARY

Other Luke had come dangerously close to spoiling my plans. He'd left me no choice – I had to get rid of him.

Not like that.

I imprisoned him in the tree house, swung by his bedroom for a super-quick change out of my Stellar costume into jeans and a jumper, then joined the rest of his – *my* – family in the car.

Fair enough, assuming the place of the Other Luke *was* a bit Evil Twin-ish, but I'd had to act fast. And in the grand scheme of things it was hardly the Anti-Monitor destroying the universe, or Bane breaking Batman's back, or Doctor Octopus taking over Spider-Man's body.

OK, it was a bit like that last one.

We arrived at the restaurant and sat down at our table. Dad was in a great mood, talking excitedly about tomorrow's launch of the new shop. Mum kept looking at him and smiling. In my world I hadn't seen them this happy for a long time. I couldn't keep the grin off my face. When I looked up from my menu I found Zack staring across at me with a curious expression.

"What are you plotting?" he said.

"Nothing."

"So what's the stupid grin about? I can tell you're up to something."

"Boys," said Mum, with the lion-taming tone in her voice.

That was close. From now on I had to be careful not to give myself away. The trick was to behave exactly like Other Luke. He would never be amused by his parents. I figured that impersonating him shouldn't be too difficult. He was just like me, only not as amazing.

After dinner Dad insisted on going for ice cream to this ancient café where he and Mum used to meet up after school when they were young. Zack said that the café probably qualified as a site of archaeological interest. Mum and Dad just held each other's hands and shared a knickerbocker glory. I didn't mind one bit that they were acting all sappy, and I wondered briefly what it would be like to stay in this world with them. But weirdly, seeing them so happy made me feel every light year of the mind-boggling distance from the family I'd left behind.

The night was over. We pulled into the driveway and with a belly full of Chinese food and ice cream I climbed contentedly out of the car.

"Where are you going?" said Mum. "Bed, mister."

I'd been heading to my usual accommodation in the tree house, having forgotten once again that I was pretending to be Other Luke. It was proving harder than I'd expected.

"Sorry, Mum, miles away," I said. And I couldn't help think how perfectly natural it felt calling her that. I wrapped my arms around her, nuzzling in close. She smelled just like my mum. So far away. I wondered if she was thinking about me too.

A cool hand touched my forehead.

"You feeling OK?"

Ten minutes later, as I prepared to slip under the duvet into my soft bed, I glanced out of the window at the dim outline of the tree house. My plan was on course, but I felt a twinge of guilt about leaving Other Luke out there, so when the house was still and everyone else was asleep, I sneaked downstairs and found the doggy bag that we'd brought back from the restaurant.

Other Luke was exactly where I'd left him, imprisoned in the tree house. A regular jailer would have used curtain tie-backs to bind his captive's wrists and ankles, and Easy Tear Scotch tape across his mouth to keep him from shouting for help. But I had no need of such crude measures. I'd used my superpowers to place an invisible force field around the tree house. Not only did it bar him from escaping and muffle any sound from within, but it also blocked all telepathic signals, preventing him from summoning Zack's help. As an added bonus, the force field kept the draught out.

"Nice and warm in here," I remarked. Other Luke studied me in silence as I opened one of the food cartons. "Lot cosier than when you stuck me here." He remained mute. "I know you don't believe me, but I am really sorry about having to lock you up like this. C'mon though – we both know you would've done the same thing, in my position."

He broke his silence. "Still sure you're not my Evil Twin?"

"Would an Evil Twin have brought you *this*?" With a flourish I offered him the carton of sweet and sour chicken.

He inspected the contents. "It's cold. And gloopy. I'm not eating that."

"You've got to eat something," I said. "Flipping heck, I

101

sound like Mum."

"She's not your mum," snapped Other Luke.

"That's arguable," I reminded him. "We're splitting hairs. Except they're not hairs, they're smaller than that. We're splitting atoms."

"That's how you make a bomb," he said accusingly. "It's called nuclear fission."

"Aha! You figured out my dastardly plan. I'm travelling from dimension to dimension rigging up the ultimate weapon that will destroy the multiverse by triggering an unstoppable chain reaction of mums."

He peered at me uncertainly. "Are you?"

"Of course not!" I fished out the prawn crackers and offered him the bag. He shook his head curtly, so I took one. He watched me hungrily as I ate.

"What do you want with my brother?" he said. "And don't tell me he's *your* brother too. Your brother is in your universe. This one is *mine*. I know you're trying to trick Zack into coming with you. But what I can't figure out is why."

"And you don't *want* to know." I wasn't discussing it. When he started to object I cut him off. "Trust me."

He let out a sarcastic laugh. He wasn't hiding his feelings, but that didn't mean I had to be unkind to him. I concentrated on a picture in my mind. There was the usual smell of chips, another tremor likely to excite a few seismologists, and a hole in the air materialised. I was getting better at this summoning thing. The ship's computer had almost blown a fuse at the last dimensional anomaly, but it hadn't specifically warned me off creating them. Anyway, one more couldn't hurt.

A toilet bowl whistled out of the hole, thudded to the floor, wobbled once and came to a standstill.

"No need for you to be uncomfortable," I said. "You'll find it all works perfectly." I pushed the flusher button and the bowl filled with water from another dimension. I had one parting shot. "Oh, and don't count on being rescued by your friends. I plan on rescheduling your regular S.C.A.R.F. meeting. Instead of the tree house, we'll get together at Serge's house for a change."

I could see his face fall. I'd outplayed him again. There wasn't much more to say, which was odd, seeing as we had so much in common. Perhaps under different circumstances we would have been friends, but I knew it could never be like that. For my mission to succeed, I would be forced to cause him great pain. Other Luke would hate me for the rest of his life. I set the food on the floor, opened a temporary hole in the force field and left.

12
USE THE FLUSH, LUKE

I paced back and forth across the tree-house floor. Stellar could fudge all he wanted, but anyone could see that he was a supervillain. Who else would turn my sanctuary into a prison? His mind was utterly twisted and he didn't even realise it: a classic supervillain characteristic. To complete the picture all he needed was a costume made of black leather and some sort of skull motif. Or maybe an octopus.

But if he thought he had the better of me, he was in for a surprise. I'd escaped tougher prisons than this. Just recently alien invaders had failed to detain me in their high-security maths classroom. Compared with that, this would be a breeze. A breeze? He was right about one thing – it felt a lot warmer in here than usual. That force field of his must be blocking the draught. Well, no amount of evil home insulation was going to prevent me from breaking out.

Three and a half hours later all I'd managed to break out was a fresh pad of A4 paper from an economy pack. I'd have preferred to escape using a clever anti-force field device that I'd cobbled together from a car battery, some fireworks and an old sledge, but I didn't have any of that stuff. I looked around at what was to hand. A stack of comics, a pack of three Pukka Pads (opened), one felt-tip pen (green), assorted novelty superhero lamps, a smoke detector, some Chinese food and an interdimensional toilet that I wasn't going near if I could help it. Earlier, I'd ventured a glance into the bowl to find it filled not with water but with swirling clouds of infinity and the distant howl of dying suns. I'd flipped down the lid smartish. I wasn't exposing any part of me to that thing.

I tugged at my collar. It wasn't just cosy in the tree house, it was hot. Never mind the draught, there wasn't a breath of air getting in here. An awful thought occurred to me: I wasn't simply imprisoned, I was *entombed*. Once I'd used up the existing air supply, I was done for. I began to gasp, even though I knew there was plenty of air left, for now. Did Stellar realise what he'd done? How evil *was* my twin? Whether by accident or design, he had sealed me in here tighter than a tuna in a can.

I decided my best course of action would be to ignore the rising panic that fluttered in my chest like a flotilla of butterflies and focus on my escape. But everything I tried came up against that impenetrable force field. If I couldn't figure a way out or Stellar didn't come back in time, then I was in deep trouble. Eventually, exhausted by my efforts, I lay down on the floor. I felt my eyelids droop. I tried to fight sleep, but I couldn't even win that battle. My last thought before I drifted off was: what's that cat doing there? Just before waves of tiredness overtook me I was convinced that I could see a cat sitting on the floor of the tree house. Actually, that's not strictly accurate, my last thought before nodding off was, randomly, I wonder which version of the Flash is the best: Barry Allen or Wally West? But the one about the cat was definitely more unexpected. I put it down to a hallucination caused by oxygen starvation – there was no way a cat or anything else could have got past the force field.

Morning came, but with it no Stellar. With a jolt I realised that it was the day of Dad's comic-shop opening and I was in danger of missing not only the big launch, but the rest of my life. The air in the tree house was definitely thinner. I decided that the important thing was to use as little of my supply as possible, which meant not exerting myself.

I leapt up with a shout as something furry touched my leg. Great – that had to be a mug-full of wasted air right there.

I looked down to find a cat sitting at my feet licking its paws. Its coat was pitch black with a single jagged white streak running along its back. I was baffled. I'd examined every centimetre of the tree house and found not even a chink in the force field, so how had it got in? I inched my way around the walls again, painstakingly searching for the cat-flap-sized hole I'd overlooked. I paused at a crack in the wall. Through it I could see across the garden and into the house. My family was in the kitchen, preparing to leave for the shop. With mounting anger I saw Stellar at the heart of things, pretending to be me. Didn't they know he was an imposter? Couldn't they see? Although I knew it was futile, I yelled to attract their attention, but as expected they continued to go about their breakfast routine. Even without the sound-dulling force field, they'd have struggled to hear me. I beat the wooden walls with my fists and was about to turn away in frustration when I glimpsed another cat in the garden. I'd almost missed it sitting there in front of Dad's shed like a shadow. I peered with growing puzzlement. It was a black cat with *exactly* the same white streak as the one in the tree house. It had to be the same animal. The cat must have slipped out without my noticing. Cursing myself for not paying attention to its escape route, I looked round only to find the creature nuzzling up to my comic stack.

I glanced out again at the cat in the garden. It sat in the same position.

The cat in the tree house. Same position.

I tried fixing one eye on the cat in the garden while continuing to observe the one in the tree house, but it was impossible to focus on both at the same time.

The obvious explanation was that there were two identical cats, but I had the oddest feeling that I was looking at the same cat in two places at once. How could that be?

I wondered. Stellar's arrival had created a great deal of disturbance in the universe, leading to the appearance of all sorts of strange phenomena. In a world suddenly filled with space-time gerbil-holes, perhaps quantum cats were only to be expected. Now that I thought about it, I remembered watching a YouTube video about a guy called Schrödinger who didn't like cats. He did this thought experiment, which meant he used the power of his mind to put a cat in a box along with some poison. And then he killed it. And also didn't kill it. At the same time. Which I suppose made him a bit like a supervillain with mind powers, like Darkseid or Ultron, although I'm not sure about their feelings towards cats. Just to be clear, no actual cats were harmed in the course of his experimenting, only imagined ones. And apparently all this mental cat-zapping effort was to prove that the universe is a very weird place.

I could've told him that.

The tree house cat sashayed to the wall.

I didn't take my eyes off it as it crossed the room, and for the first time I noticed that it was wearing a collar with a small round tag. A shaft of morning light flashed against the metal circle, illuminating a single letter "Z". What did it stand for? Zack? Zatanna? Zoom? What about *Zorbon*? Had he sent the cat, and if so, why? As I pondered the question, the cat squeezed through a gap that seemed far too small for its sinewy body and slunk out. There was a fizz of protest from the force field but the cat didn't seem to notice. It was already on the other side, having broken through Stellar's barrier without raising a hackle. When I looked into the garden, I could only see one cat. Now, that *was* weird.

It was then that I remembered what Lara had said

about cats. They were not like other creatures. Cats were uncontrollable. Not even her Dark Flutter animal powers could convince the most ordinary, domestic moggie to do anything it didn't want to do. Was it possible that cats were immune to superpowers?

Either way, the passage of this one through the force field had certainly disrupted the invisible barrier, which continued to buzz and pop for a few seconds. That gave me an idea – what if I could overload the force field and make it crash? I just needed something to shove in the field that would cause a short circuit. But I was all out of cats.

The dimensional toilet gurgled with the whoosh of a gamma-ray burst.

Of course! Crouching down next to it, I wrapped my arms around the base of the bowl, counted to three and then gave a great heave. It was a lot heavier than I'd counted on – maybe because of all those supermassive stars I'd glimpsed inside. I staggered about the tree house, my muscles burning as I lugged it to the door. With my ear so close to the porcelain bowl I was sure I could hear infinity sloshing about inside. I got into position. I was Luke Skywalker targeting the Death Star's thermal exhaust port, except that instead of a proton torpedo, I had a toilet.

Rocking on my heels I began to swing the toilet bowl back and forth to build up momentum. When I judged that I had enough force, I let go. It sailed through the air, straight and true. A split second later the door splintered before its porcelain power, and then it impacted against the force field. A direct hit! One in a million, kid! There was a furious crackle accompanied by a shower of sparks and then silence.

To my relief I felt a welcome gust of cold air sweep inside. There was no way of telling whether the force field was down for good, so, seizing my chance, I hurried out.

The house was locked up. Stellar and my family had already left for the comic shop. No matter. Stellar had underestimated me. Without the barrier of the force field I was free to contact Zack telepathically. In my head I formed the words: "Zack, can you hear me? There is no Gorgon the World-Eater. He's really Gordon, and he's one of my supervillain Top Trump cards. Stellar's trying to trick you. Come in. Over."

I waited for his response. At first there was only empty static, then a voice broke through the silence. But it wasn't my brother.

"Place the strawberries in the bowl and gently toss through the sugar. Leave uncovered at room temperature

111

overnight. This process helps the sugar to dissolve, ensuring that the fruit doesn't disintegrate too much and helping to keep its colour…"

Stellar was jamming the signal.

He was one step ahead of me yet again. I set off at a run for the bus stop, vowing that the next time we came face to face I wouldn't come off second best. I drew out my bus pass. It was time for the final confrontation with my Evil Twin.

13
A FISTFUL OF MACAROONS

So far so good. Other Luke wasn't going anywhere and I'd fooled Mum and Dad into believing I was him. Zack's initial doubts about me had vanished into thin air after a simple argument over Shredded Wheat. It left him in no doubt that he was talking to his irritating younger brother.

The short car journey into town passed with great excitement. We arrived at the shop and set about making final preparations for the grand reopening. As the others went inside I paused to check out the sign that hung above the front window. In bold yellow letters with a red drop-shadow against a dark-blue background it read: *Parker & Sons – Your Friendly Neighbourhood Comic Store.*

"& Sons". Reading the words, I felt a spasm of guilt like a stitch in my side. I quashed it back down. My mission was all that mattered. I followed the others inside.

"In the words of 80s poodle-rockers Europe," said Dad, switching on all the lights and firing up the superhero musical carousel, "it's the final countdown."

Soon the doors would be flung wide to welcome Parker & Sons' first customers. I glanced up at the Kang the Conqueror wall clock that hung over the cash register. I had to keep up my pretence for a few more hours. Could I fool Other Luke's family and friends for that long? Only time – and Kang – would tell.

Mum and Zack went down to the basement to sort out the Dark Flutter themed petting zoo while Dad and I busied ourselves upstairs with some light shelf-dusting. He paused next to the big front window and stared out.

"What are you looking at?" I asked him.

"Nothing," said Dad. "I was hoping for a line of customers around the block." His tone grew anxious. "Maybe I should've bought a car for everyone in Bromley, or banned someone famous. Y'know, a publicity stunt." He rested his forehead on the glass and sighed. "Oh, Luke, what I wouldn't give for Star Lad to make an appearance."

That wasn't going to happen. The plan was for us to

rendezvous later at IKEA.

The front door opened and Serge staggered in wearing a green and yellow superhero costume, holding a wobbling stack of Tupperware boxes. Perched on the topmost box was a baguette filled with spanners.

"Are you dressed as Matter-Eater Lad?" I asked.

Serge poked his head out from behind the tower of plastic boxes.

"*Oui*, so are you going to don the cape of Star Lad?"

"No, I'm Ste—" I caught myself just in time. "Ste-pping over here to do this." I shuffled a few comics on a nearby shelf.

"Serge, you're awesome," said Dad, taking the boxes from him and laying them down on the counter.

Besides dressing up as a member of the Legion of Super-Heroes, Serge's other contribution to today's event turned out to be a marathon baking session. Dad and Serge unpacked the contents of the boxes and soon, ranged along the counter, were trays piled high with glossy multicoloured patisseries.

Serge examined them with a critical eye. "I had hoped to achieve a Fortress of Solitude structure in the presentation of my *macarons* but in the end settled for these simple but elegant pyramids."

Dad made some approving response but I couldn't tell

what he was saying since his mouth was crammed with *macaron*. "Right, I'll be back in five," he said when he'd gulped down the last morsel. "Got to change into my costume."

There was a ping from the lift in the middle of the shop. The doors slid apart and out walked Zack and Mum. She wore a costume I didn't recognise. Green tights, thigh boots, a green top with a wooden dagger tucked at her hip, and a hat shaped like a paper boat.

"If you're meant to be Green Arrow, where's your bow?" I asked.

"I'm Peter Pan!" she said brightly and then for some reason slapped her thigh.

I should've guessed. Back in the days when Dad turned nursery rhymes into space opera, Mum preferred to stick to the classics. Her favourite was Peter Pan. Though it always made her cry.

This was embarrassing for her. "Uh, sorry, but Peter Pan's not a superhero," I said.

"Uh, sorry," she mimicked me, "but he can fly, he's immortal and he has the power to travel between worlds." She turned to Dad. "I could do with some help downstairs. One of the rabbits won't wear her helmet. Come on, follow me."

Dad clutched a hand dramatically to his chest. "But,

Peter, what if I fall?"

"What if you fly?" She spun on her heel and stuck out a finger. "Second star to the right, and straight on till morning."

From what I could remember, those were the directions to Neverland, not the basement. Nevertheless, with that the two of them skipped off happily together.

"Apart from the occasional uncooperative bunny," said Zack when they'd gone, "it all seems to be coming together remarkably well." He shot me a look. "Where's your costume? Surely you of all people aren't going to miss an opportunity to dress up as some obscure superhero."

I'd forgotten how annoying Zack could be.

"These macaroon things are yummy, Serge," he said, chewing on one.

"*Merci*, Zack." He lowered his voice. "And may I, in my capacity as co-founder and chief logo designer of S.C.A.R.F., enquire as to whether you are fully prepared for your forthcoming cross-dimensional mission?"

"Yup, all set—" I began, before realising the question wasn't addressed to me.

Zack tutted. "You're not coming along on this one, remember?"

Oops. "Oh yeah, must've slipped my non-superpowered mind."

"Are you feeling quite all right, *mon ami*? You seem to be particularly jumpy today."

"Me – jumpy? Skittish? Jittery? I think not, Serge. I've never felt more mentally stable in my entire life." I could feel their puzzled expressions boring into me. To my relief, just then Lara arrived. I hurried off to open the door.

"What have you come as?" I asked as she swept in to the shop. Her costume consisted of normal, boring clothes, a spiral-bound notebook and what looked suspiciously like a fine-point Uni-ball pen.

"Lois Lane, obviously," she said. "I couldn't exactly show up as Dark Flutter, could I?"

We joined Serge and Zack in the S.C.A.R.F. huddle.

"Hi, Serge," said Lara.

"Ah, *bonjour*, Lara. Or should I say … *Lois*?"

Really? He got that from a notebook?

"Will you be accompanying Star Lad on the mission to Stellar's universe?" Serge asked.

"That's the plan," said Lara. "Mum thinks I'm staying at her house and Dad thinks I'm at his. I reckon I've got three days until either of them notices I've gone. And this way I'll be able to keep a close eye on Stellar." She turned to me. "Did you dig up any dirt on him?"

She was asking *me* about Stellar? "Uh, no, not a superpowered sausage," I said, trying to sound disappointed, but inside I was grinning from ear to ear. I had fooled the lot of them. Regrettably I was forced to keep my brilliance to myself.

"Me neither," said Lara. "Is it possible we were wrong about him? After all, he is you, and you're not evil."

"Of course Stellar's not evil," I objected. "He's amazing." The others stared at me. Perhaps I'd overdone the compliment thing. "Amazing at being a pain," I added in an attempt to cover up my slip.

Lara and Serge nodded a bit too readily for my liking.

"I agree," said Zack. "I've spent more time with him than any of you lot and, just between us, he's always trying to suck up. He's ... what's the word?"

"Creepy?" suggested Lara.

"Unctuous?" said Serge.

"Misunderstood?" I offered.

Ouch. Pretending to be someone else meant that people could be unnecessarily harsh about you when they thought you weren't around.

"You will be careful, won't you?" said Serge.

This time I didn't make the mistake of answering, as I could see he was addressing Lara. She still believed that she was coming on the mission.

"Don't worry," she said to Serge. "You're not getting rid of me that easily. I'm like a boomerang."

"Or perhaps a Batarang?" suggested Serge.

Lara looked confused. "What's a Batarang?"

I expected Serge to react the way any normal person would when faced with such a response: that is, roll his eyes, throw his arms up and say, "How could you not know about Batman's classic throwing weapon?" To my astonishment, Serge didn't do any of that. Instead he said it was unimportant (*unimportant?!*), and then Lara noticed the macaroons on the counter.

"Are these yours?" she said, casting an eye over the colourful display.

"*Oui*, although I must confess that my *maman* helped me to achieve the sophisticated, glossy finish."

She plucked a red one between a finger and thumb. "Beautiful, and so light – like little coloured clouds. Do you think you could teach me how to make them?"

Serge raised an eyebrow. "I should be delighted." He took a step towards her and in a low voice said, "The trick is to bake them until they are set, but not browned."

"Yes," said Lara, gazing into his eyes.

He moved closer. "The crunch on the outside conceals a yielding, squashy inside."

"Yes," she repeated in a weird breathy voice.

I knew they were talking about macaroons, but I had the oddest feeling that there was another conversation going on between the words. Not that I had the first idea what it might be about.

The two of them stood quite still, watching one another in silence, apparently lost in their own little world.

"So," murmured Serge at last, "your kitchen or mine?"

I didn't hear Lara's answer because at that moment I was distracted by a dull throbbing in the spot directly between my eyes. It was my Stellar Scanner, a radar in my head that alerted me to important activity happening nearby. I closed my eyes and concentrated, trying to visualise what had set it off.

Other Luke marched along the High Street, heading for the comic shop.

14
THE TRANS-DIMENSIONAL CARROT TEMPTATION

By the time I arrived at the shop a queue had formed on the pavement outside. Not a queue like you'd get for a new *Star Wars* film – I could count this lot on the fingers of Luke Skywalker's one real hand. Josh Khan was among them, wearing a rubbish homemade costume consisting of a dorsal fin and a pair of stubby wings. I breezed past before he saw me and, ignoring shouts of outrage from the others, strode through the front door.

I found Zack, Serge and Lara clustered around the cash register, preparing for the imminent opening. Zack was emptying packets of coins into the till while Serge sorted through a display of comics filled entirely with variant covers. Before I could demand where Stellar was, Lara spoke up.

"Did you find them?" she said.

"Find what?"

"You said that you felt a pain in the neck creeping up on you, so you went looking for headache pills."

So Stellar must have detected my arrival and hotfooted it out of sight. He couldn't have gone far. "That wasn't me, it was Stellar." I stuck my head round the nearest display case. "Which way did he go?"

"It can't have been him. Lara and I are meeting up with him later," said Zack. "He's waiting for us at IKEA."

That threw me. "Your rendezvous point is IKEA? Y'know what, that doesn't matter right now. He isn't there. He's here and he looks *exactly* like me."

"Of course he does," said Zack with a sigh. "We've established that."

Gah! "He's *pretending* to be me!"

"Luke, we've been through this," said Lara.

"Yeah, why on earth would he do that?" said Zack.

"Because I found a homemade Top Trump card that proves he's up to no good and he imprisoned me in the tree house with a force field that I managed to deactivate this morning with a pair of quantum cats and an interdimensional toilet."

Zack's features formed an expression with which I had become all too familiar, namely weary disbelief. Thankfully I could see the other two members of S.C.A.R.F. absorb this new information with the seriousness it deserved. I explained all about the fictional supervillain called Gordon the World-Eater.

"So you see, Gordon is just a carrot," I said at last.

"A carrot?" said Zack.

"Yeah, y'know – a temptation."

Zack looked puzzled. "But I don't like carrots."

"No one likes carrots. That's not the point."

My brother had roundly dismissed my explanation, but I held out hope that my S.C.A.R.F. colleagues would believe me.

"Serge?"

"You have not one shred of evidence and you come here with a story that relies upon unlikely cats and fantastical sanitary ware." He paused. "I believe you one hundred per cent."

"Me too," said Lara. "Though I'd put it about seventy-five per cent."

Zack gave her a pained look.

I knew I could count on them! Just then Mum and Dad returned from the basement, forcing me to draw a temporary halt to my Stellar hunt. I couldn't exactly ask them if they'd seen someone who looked exactly like me strolling around the shop in search of Calpol. Mum was holding a rabbit wearing an orange mask and a cape with a carrot sigil. Her own costume puzzled me. "If you're meant to be Green Arrow," I said, "where's your bow?"

She gave me this funny look. "I told you already, I'm Peter Pan."

It took me a second to understand her choice, but then I got it. I clicked my fingers. "He can fly, he lives forever and he can travel across dimensions. Brilliant!"

Mum ignored me and stroked the rabbit. "Commander Cottontail won't play nicely with the rest of the Green Lettuce Corps."

It twitched its pink nose and made a low, sighing noise.

"His mask is pinching his ears," Lara explained, before quickly adding, "Uh, I mean it looks a bit tight, don't you think?" She fiddled with the elastic and avoided Mum's curious gaze.

Zack looked Dad up and down. "And who are you meant to be?"

Serge and I exchanged disbelieving looks – how did Zack even manage to get out of bed in the morning with such a dismal knowledge of superheroes? It was *obvious* who Dad had come as. Instead of some variant of Superman, in the end he had plumped for Superman's dad, Jor-El. He'd copied the costume worn by the character in the ancient film that came out in 1978, which consisted of the brightest white tunic and trousers in the known universe. He wore a wig of equally dazzling white hair, with a curl that hung down in the centre of his forehead. To complete the look he'd strapped a plastic baby into a harness on his chest.

"I'll give you a clue," said Dad. He cradled the doll and began talking to it in a voice that sounded like his cheeks were filled with cotton-wool balls. "They can be a great people, Kal-El. They only lack the light to show them. For this reason above all, their capacity for good, I have sent them you ... my only son."

Zack shook his head. "No idea," he said, and wandered off.

Serge clapped appreciatively. "Bravo, Monsieur Parker. *Superbe*. I felt I was right there with you on the doomed Krypton."

"Thanks, Serge. That moment when the planet is disintegrating about him and Jor-El has to send his baby boy off in the spaceship so that he'll survive." He put on the voice again. *"Goodbye, my son."* Dad sniffed. "Gets me every time." He flicked at his white curl and marched to the door. "Now, that's what I call a queue."

The handful of customers who'd been waiting when

I arrived had swelled. There were now so many that they'd spilled into the street. Dad flipped over the sign from "CLOSED TIME LOOP" to "HAILING FREQUENCY OPEN".

"Brace for impact," he said, rubbing his hands together.

The queue didn't move.

When after a few seconds still no one had entered the shop, Dad peered out at the stationary customers. "What are they waiting for?"

It was then I noticed that they were all looking up. I craned my neck to see what had gripped their attention and glimpsed a shape flitting between the buildings. A snatch of a cape confirmed my suspicion.

"Stellar," I muttered under my breath, and went outside for a better look. The others followed me on to the street.

I caught sight of him immediately, circling low over the comic shop, cape rippling *just so*, shoes shining like paint on a really expensive German car. I swear even his teeth sparkled in the sunlight. It seemed as if every shop on the High Street had emptied of people, and all of them were massing outside Parker & Sons, goggling at the aerobatic display my superhero double had decided to put on.

"Well, how about that," cooed Dad. "There's a new player in town."

"Oh, he's very impressive, isn't he?" said Mum, her eyes fixed skyward.

"But you don't even like superheroes," I complained.

"Yes, I know, sweetheart, but *he* is something special." She waved up at Stellar. "You can just tell."

Even my own mum was a fan. This was getting beyond a joke.

"More special than Star Lad?" asked Zack. His voice quivered, but Mum didn't hear him over the noise of the excited crowd.

They whooped and cheered as Stellar reached the climax of his routine. Not content with endlessly circling, he proceeded to perform a total show-off move, executing a supersonic half-loop off the top of a subsonic barrel-roll. Cries of admiration rising to meet him, he touched down on the roof of the comic shop and, with the poise of a tightrope walker, strode to the edge. He positioned himself directly above the sign and raised his arms to the crowd. They fell obediently silent.

"Greetings, citizens of Bromley *Two*." He held up two fingers, in case there was any doubt. "I am Stellar."

The crowd oohed and aahed.

"Good name," said Dad with a firm nod.

"I come to you from another world, beyond your galaxy, beyond your universe, beyond *understanding*." He knelt down on one knee and swept an arm to the far horizon. His performance was turning into an interpretative dance. Slowly he raised his chin. "And I am here with a *vital* message."

15
WHEN LUKES COLLIDE

Stellar paused, and in the silence that followed I could sense the crowd straining to hear his next words. I knew what was coming, of course. This was the moment when he crowed his plans for world domination and revealed himself as the supervillain I'd had him pegged as right from the beginning.

He cleared his throat. "Whenever I'm in a parallel universe, I buy all my comics at Parker & Sons – Your Friendly Neighbourhood Comic Store."

What? What did he say? I looked at the others for confirmation, sure that I must have misheard. But I hadn't.

Dad cheered.

The crowd cheered.

I shook my head in disgust. "That's outrageous. That's blatant commercialism. That's—"

My further objections were drowned out by the noisy crowd. It seemed that, unlike me, they wholeheartedly approved.

Stellar marched up and down the roof. "And today only," he shouted above the roar, "every purchase you make at Parker & Sons enters you into a unique prize draw. You could win a superpowered flight of a lifetime, courtesy of *me*. Minimum spend of ten pounds. Terms and conditions apply."

I tutted my disapproval. "OK, now he's just getting carried away."

"Didn't you ask me to do much the same thing?" asked Zack.

"No. Well, yes, but that was different," I stuttered. It was one thing suggesting to Zack that he promote the shop, quite another to watch Stellar hog the limelight.

There was a thunder of feet on the pavement as, spurred by his offer, what seemed like the entire population of Bromley descended on the shop.

"Come on," cried Dad, leading the charge inside.

"It's overdraft-clobbering time!"

Suddenly I was yanked off my feet. An overly excited Josh Khan grabbed me by the shoulders and stared wide-eyed into my face at a distance close enough to tell precisely which kind of cheese flavoured the cheese and onion crisps he'd just scoffed.

"Did you hear that?" His grip tightened. "I'm going to fly with Dark Flutter."

"Uh, were you even listening?" I looked him up and down. "And who exactly are you meant to be?"

"I'm Shark Flutter," he said proudly, explaining that it was a superhero of his own invention. As far as I could gather from his breathless origin story, the character was half Great White, half humming-bird, and Dark Flutter's best friend. I couldn't help notice that his cape kept snagging on his fin. I was about to tell him that a shark that big getting airborne with those wings was an aerodynamic impossibility, but he had already gone, haring after the others into the shop. I brushed down my rumpled sleeves.

"It's time to leave," announced Zack. "Stellar just contacted me telepathically. He's moving up our departure."

"But what about the free flight offer?" I said.

Zack tutted and turned to Lara. "You all set?"

"Wait! No, you can't go." I laid a hand on my brother's arm.

"I know what you're going to say," he said wearily. "That Stellar's only pretending to be a superhero. That he's really a supervillain. But would a supervillain help promote Dad's comic shop?"

I thought for a moment. "Probably not Galactus, no. The Joker might. Lex Luthor definitely would, for a fee."

Serge mumbled his agreement.

Zack sighed. "Face it, Luke, you're wrong about Stellar." He reached into a pocket for his wallet and removed what looked like a credit card. "You have been from the start."

Just when I was thinking that he was too young to have a credit card, I noticed that the card was emblazoned with his Star Lad sigil. Weird. I was about to quiz him about it when he signalled to Lara.

"Dark Flutter, let's suit up."

"Right behind you," said Lara. "Look after this for me while I'm gone." She handed me her precious phone. "I don't want to risk taking it with me to another dimension."

I nodded in complete understanding. "In case it falls into the hands of a supervillain who uses the information contained on your SIM to discover your true identity and wreak havoc with your life?"

"No." She frowned. "Roaming charges."

I pocketed the phone and watched them as they headed off through the crowd for somewhere less public to change into their superhero outfits. They each had cover stories for their absence. As far as Mum and Dad were concerned, their eldest son would be boarding a chartered school bus, along with the rest of the track and field team, for three days of intensive coaching at Professor Xavier's Academy for Gifted Youngsters. (OK, it wasn't actually named after the X-Men's secret school. It had some boring, sporty name, which I've forgotten.)

I felt helpless but what could I do? As I considered my diminishing options, an idea struck me. I had one more card to play.

"Serge, follow me," I said, turning back to the shop. By then the queue was like a zombie uprising. Hundreds of grunting bodies pressed through the front door. Squeezing past them, we fought our way up to the roof. I shouldered my way through the access door and, with relief, saw Stellar peering down at the line of customers snaking all the way along the High Street.

He gave a self-satisfied nod. "Pretty effective bit of advertising, even if I say so myself." His expression darkened. "Though it won't matter in the end. Dad won't care. None of you will."

I barely registered his words – I was too angry with him. "I almost suffocated. You could've killed me, locking me up like that."

"I'm sorry. I didn't mean to."

It sounded as if he meant it. There was a ripple of excitement from the crowd below. They'd just noticed Star Lad and Dark Flutter descending from the sky to join Stellar on the roof.

"Ready when you are, Ste—" Zack broke off when he saw me. "What are *you* doing here?"

"I'm in the middle of a showdown with my Evil Twin," I huffed.

"Well, you and Serge can't be up here. There are health and safety issues." He counted off on his fingers. "This area lacks a safety rail. Those roof lights constitute a falling hazard. Neither of you can fly—"

"Zack, give it a rest. I'm not going to fall off the roof, not unless *he* pushes me." I pointed a rigid finger at Stellar. "And have you asked him what he's doing here? If there's now such a pressing need to fight Gorgon the World-Eater, why's he wasting time flying over our shop, making speeches and drumming up business?"

I could tell from Zack's reaction that I'd scored a point,

but before he could turn the question on Stellar, my Evil Twin spoke up.

"I knew it might look odd, me showing up at the comic shop when we'd arranged our rendezvous for later," he said, "but I wanted to help Dad. Before I left."

"He's not your dad," I snapped. "And what's with the rendezvous point? I mean seriously, IKEA?"

"They're big, easy to spot from a long way off and there's an IKEA in every universe," he answered briskly. "They're sort of like portals. Big blue portals. With meatballs."

Actually, that made a lot of sense. Darn it, he had an answer for everything. So instead of going after Stellar, I shifted my aim to Zack.

"Lara and Serge can see that he's lying; why can't you?" Even as I posed the question, I knew the answer. Zack was terrible at seeing through lies. I think it's because he always hoped for the best in people. "For the last time, there is no Gorgon the World-Eater or *Gordon* the World-Eater," I said. "He's a big, fat made-up supervillain." I was conscious that my voice had gone up a notch and that I sounded like a screechy choirboy.

"No, he isn't," responded Stellar.

"Yes, he is."

"No, he isn't."

Zack stepped in between us like an umpire in a tennis match. "Enough!"

I glowered at Stellar. "Well, one of us is lying and it's not me."

"And it's definitely not me," he snapped back.

There was only one way to resolve the situation. "Zack, you have to choose between us."

"So who do you believe?" said Stellar.

"Me?"

"Or him?"

I could see Zack's gaze move between us. Luke or *Luke*?

"Aggh! One of you was bad enough, but this is impossible! Stellar, why are you even arguing with him? Gorgon the World-Eater is a fact, right?"

I detected a hint of uncertainty in my brother's voice. Stellar had heard it too. Something in his expression changed.

"He's real. Of course he's real," he protested. "Why would I make up something like that?"

I pounced. "Aha! And *that's* the burning question. So why did you?"

We were eye to eye, a mirror image of each other, except that it was an evil mirror belonging to some dastardly fairytale queen. I was close enough to count his nose-hairs, but that wasn't why I had brilliantly manoeuvred myself into this position.

I had a plan.

Superhero costumes are notorious for their lack of storage. When I'd helped Lara design hers I'd ensured that it included a number of easily accessible pockets, but with the exception of Dark Flutter – and Batman with his utility belt – most superheroes would struggle to pocket a two-finger Kit-Kat. I scoured Stellar's costume. There was a single zip pocket at his chest, neatly concealed by the line of his starburst sigil.

If he had the Top Trump card on him, it was in there.

Flexing my fingers I prepared for the most important sleight of hand since Mandrake the Magician pulled his first rabbit out of a hat.

I glanced up. "Ooh, is that Zorbon's ship up there?"

All eyes turned to scan the empty sky. With everyone's attention on the non-existent craft, my fingers brushed Stellar's zip then dipped into the pocket. One, two …
Abraca-whammo!

"Got you!" I had it. The card was back in my possession. I thrust it in front of Zack's face. "See, I told you. I told you he wasn't real."

As Zack inspected the Top Trump, I watched the colour drain from Stellar's face.

"He is real," Stellar mumbled weakly.

His plan was in tatters. I almost felt sorry for him. He could complain all he wanted; I had won. In the end, good had triumphed over evil, just as it always did.

Stellar's tone hardened, he balled his hands into fists and kept repeating, "He is real. He is. HE IS!"

"There's no point having a tantrum," I said. "C'mon now, no hard feelings. Face it, you were outplayed by the better—"

"Look!" cried Lara.

Something was happening above the far end of the High Street. As I squinted at what appeared to be a crack in the sky, the air filled with an aroma like ten thousand sizzling deep-fat fryers.

"It is *une gerbille-*'ole," breathed Serge.

In seconds it swelled from a jagged tear to something the size of a thundercloud. The sky darkened as the hole grew. And grew. A shape formed, its outline unmistakable. I should know, since I had drawn it. Dread gripped me, as dark as an eclipse. The outline filled up. Now it was something solid. Something utterly monstrous. It put one leg down and the ground shook like the earth had been hit by a wrecking-ball the size of the moon.

Gordon the World-Eater stepped into the universe.

16
ARMAGORDON

Everything is true in the multiverse: gerbils with laser-eyes, rocket shoes and now this. Gordon the World-Eater was just as I – and Stellar – had drawn him all those years ago. He towered thirty storeys high in a pair of winged sandals, standing on legs as big as battleships. He had a ridiculously muscled torso impervious to all attacks, including magic, nuclear missiles and wasps (I remember having been stung by one around the time of his creation). Back when I'd drawn him I hadn't understood that planets don't twinkle, only stars. So, to be accurate, he ought to have been called the star-eater. Standing there on the roof of the comic shop I realised with horror that I'd accidentally purpose-built him to defeat Star Lad.

But *I* wasn't the one who'd summoned him through a dimensional portal. I turned my furious gaze on Stellar, who met it with a sheepish expression.

"Oops."

"Oops? OOPS?!"

"It's not my fault," he hissed. "I wouldn't have been thinking about Gordon and I wouldn't have accidentally, y'know, brought him into existence, if *you* hadn't provoked me."

"Me?! Don't try pinning this on me."

He put on a whiny voice. "Gordon's not real, Gordon's a Top Trump. You wouldn't stop bugging me."

"Hate to interrupt," said Zack. "But, umm, giant unstoppable supervillain about to destroy the world?"

"There goes the Glades," said Lara.

The shopping centre took a direct hit from one of Gordon's many destructor beams, which was unfortunate for a lot of reasons, one being that it had only just reopened following Star Lad's battle in the Food Court with a giant alien robot last month. It went up in a shower of glass, brick and fast-moving consumer goods.

"Leave this to me," said Stellar. "I brought him here;

I can send him back."

So saying, he closed his eyes and focused every fibre of his superpowered being on the task. His whole body shook with the effort. Sweat poured from his forehead. The veins at his temple throbbed.

His eyes still squeezed tightly shut, Stellar's voice came out in a strained whisper. "Tell me when he's been dragged back into the dimensional void by my irresistible vortex of cosmic power."

"Not yet," said Zack.

"How about now?" grunted Stellar.

"Um, no. Sorry."

"He just stomped on Nandos," I added.

Stellar opened his eyes. "Oh bum."

He had failed to banish the World-Eater back to the weird Top Trump dimension from which he'd come. Gordon was firmly in our world now, and judging by his reaction, he wasn't a fan. He scythed his way along the High Street, causing devastation with each giant step.

"We have to lead him away from the population centre," said Zack. "But first I need to know exactly what we're dealing with."

I held up the Top Trump card and the others clustered around. "Strength 100, Speed 100, Psionic Ability 100, Healing Power 10."

"Aha!" Zack seized on the last number. "So there's a chink in his armour. A weakness we can exploit."

"Oh no, wait," I said, re-examining the card. "It's a bit smudged. It's not 10 … it's 100."

Zack snatched the card from my hand and began to read aloud. "Fire-breath, invisibility, poison toes, cyclone breath – wait, he's got that *and* fire-breath?" He shook his head in disbelief. "At least now we know what we're up against."

"Uh, no. There's more," I said. "On the back."

Zack flipped the card over. The list continued in three columns. "Night vision, X-ray vision, Laser vision. Heat ray, Freeze ray, Shrink ray. Energy Field. Energy Beam. Energy drink. Magnetism. Animal magnetism. Oh, and he has a Ring of Power. Great. What powers *didn't* you give him?"

"Flying," I said.

"OK, at least there's that."

The sky turned stormy, flashes of lightning lit up the buildings, and Gordon the World-Eater materialised next to the comic shop.

"Uh, that's because you don't need flight," I confessed, "if you've got teleportation."

Zack triggered his force field just as Gordon let loose with a barrage of the aforementioned powers. The freeze ray and heat ray bounced off the protective field, but it began to weaken following a one-two punch of cyclone breath and fire breath. Zack staggered back, scrabbling for grip on the surface of the roof.

Stellar added his powers to Zack's. The force field held, but it soon became clear that even together they couldn't withstand Gordon indefinitely. At some point, they would be overcome. It was only a matter of time.

In quick succession two sonic booms pealed across the churning sky as a pair of alert fighters swooped down to engage the invader. Earth's defence forces had detected the threat and sent a welcoming committee.

"They got here fast," I remarked.

"Star Squad Six," said Zack.

"What Squad Who?"

"After the business with Nemesis and the sue-dunham invasion, the military top brass got in touch," Zack explained. "I've been working with them to set up quick-reaction forces across the country."

"When? In between your mocks?"

He ignored me and continued to outline their Star Lad-specific role. "There are eight specialist squads consisting of personnel and equipment drawn from every branch of the military, whose job is to coordinate with me when the world is under threat."

I felt a bit put out at this latest development. "You mean like S.C.A.R.F.?"

I didn't hear Zack's response, since at that moment the fighter jets' look-down shoot-down radars identified the hostile and guided missiles leapt from their wings to home in on the target with unerring accuracy.

Gordon the World-Eater spun round to deal with this new threat. Instead of dodging the missiles or intercepting them with one of his many beam-based weapons, he stood and waited directly in their path. They flew into the black hole that I'd drawn for his head and disappeared. There followed two faint explosions that sounded a lot like crunches. If I wasn't mistaken, he'd eaten the missiles.

"Their weapons are useless," declared Zack.

Seriously? Had he expected anything else?

The jets circled about for a second run, this time lighting up the sky with cannon fire.

"When you were creating this thing, you did give him a fatal flaw, right?" Zack yelled above the onslaught.

"You mean like kryptonite?"

"Exactly. But at this point I'd take a nut allergy."

I shook my head. "Whoever held the Gordon the World-Eater card won the game. Always. He's unbeatable."

Stellar moved to the edge of the roof with a look of determination. "Then I guess we'll have to do this the hard way."

Before any of us could stop him, he had launched himself into the air.

"Little fool!" yelled Zack. "He's going to get himself killed."

Stellar streaked towards Gordon, a superpowered missile, locked on and unstoppable. Gordon's heat ray bloomed, then his energy beam lanced across the sky. Stellar swerved, gracefully dodging each attack. He was closing in fast.

"He's going to do it!" muttered Lara in amazement.

Even I was impressed – my Evil Twin had some moves.

But then with a lazy swipe from one of his double-decker-sized hands, Gordon the World-Eater batted Stellar away like a bothersome fly, sending him spinning across the roofs of the High Street.

"Superhero down!" cried Serge.

17
GET TO THE CHOPPER!

Stellar was down, but was he out? At that moment I had no way of knowing. I looked up as the beat of rotor-blades filled the air and a swarm of transport helicopters thundered low over the High Street, angling in for a landing. I counted at least six dual-rotor Chinooks. The leader broadcast a message: "Shoppers, prepare for immediate evacuation."

Even Star Squad Six couldn't have foreseen the threat of a thirty-storey world-devouring terror crashing through the main shopping street, so this was an impressively speedy response. The helicopters touched down, military personnel jumped out and began to steer people towards the transports.

It didn't take long for Gordon to sense their presence. I hadn't given him eyes, but he had a range of abilities that allowed him to detect even the merest vibration. He lowered his great head to investigate. It hung like a black sun over the nearest helicopter. At the sight of the monster, the pilot decided to take off in a hurry.

"They're not going to make it," said Zack. "Not without help."

"My turn," said Lara. With a squawk, she leapt from the roof. As she reached the top of her jump, a flock of birds swooped in and latched themselves on to her cape. She flew off swiftly in the direction of a dark cloud. For a moment I thought it was another gerbil-hole, but it was moving this way. Fast. As it drew closer I realised what I was watching.

Lara returned – at the centre of the biggest flock of birds I'd ever seen. There had to be thousands of tiny fluttering…

"Starlings?" said Serge. "What does she think that she is doing? This is madness."

The flock dived and swooped together, one great feathered mass, turning the air into vast black curves.

Under Lara's control, the flock began to form a new shape. It stretched and flailed, bent and twisted, like some nightmare creature trying to escape from quicksand, until at last its final form emerged. Even though I knew it was made entirely of tiny birds, the effect was striking. It appeared to be a creature, bigger than two titanosaurs glued together. Spikes ran the length of its crooked back; arms ended in hands that were whirling black blades; its legs were the size of skyscrapers. It dwarfed Gordon the World-Eater.

Zack assessed the situation with a practised eye. "There's only one thing a predator like Gordon the World-Eater is afraid of. And that's a predator further up the food chain."

The Lara-beast roared. A tweeting bird is not exactly a frightening sound, but let me tell you that when thousands of them sing out at once it makes quite an impression. Gordon reared up, lifting his head away from the helicopter, gazing into the face of what, to him, must have appeared to be a terrifying rival. Lara's decoy plan was working. With another tweet of terror, she marched her bird-monster towards Gordon. He took a cautious step back.

That was all the space the helicopter pilot needed. He banked his aircraft and, engines straining, gunned it out of harm's way.

Gordon wasn't fooled for long. Puffing out his

cheeks, he blew a dose of cyclone breath through the flock, breaking the formation, scattering birds across the sky. Caught up in the blast, Lara whirled through the air. Calling her feathered friends to her once more, she righted herself and was back in business. But before she could launch a fresh attack, Gordon vanished. One second he was there, blotting out the sun, the next he had gone.

"She's done it!" yelled Serge. "She has vanquished him. *Vive la* Dark Flutter!" He took a celebratory puff of his asthma inhaler.

I wasn't so sure. "He's still here," I said. "Only now he's invisible."

I scanned the sky for a sign. The thing about invisibility was that it didn't make you undetectable. Which meant that even an invisible supervillain would leave a trace of his passing. Was that a ripple in the air? A shadow across the sun?

"Well, he's gone for now. Which gives us time to regroup," said Zack. "I should contact Star Squad Six—"

The door to the roof banged open. Mum and Dad tumbled out, followed by Josh Khan. He jabbed a finger at me.

"I told you I saw him go up here."

My parents froze, trying to take in the puzzling sight

that greeted them.

"Luke?" said Mum.

"Star Lad?" said Dad.

I could appreciate their confusion. What they saw was their youngest son, his best friend and the world's greatest superhero. I thought they dealt with the situation remarkably well.

"Mr Parker, I am *mucho* impressed," cooed Josh. "I mean first that new kid Stellar shows up and does his thing, then there's the giant monster thingy with the rays and the breath and the other thingies." He lumbered about in an imitation of Gordon the World-Eater. "Then to top that you get Dark Flutter to do her totally awesome bird thingy. And now, just when we think it's all over, here's Star Lad, in super-person! And the Crowd. Goes. Wild. Yaaaah!" He raised his fists and pumped the air, while jogging around the roof in some sort of weird victory dance.

Dad threw a questioning look at Mum.

"He thinks you organised all this to advertise the shop," she explained, and immediately turned to me. "Luke, where's your brother?"

I glanced at Zack. "Um…"

He adjusted his mask. "Last time I saw him he was with that girl, Lara. They were heading for the helicopters."

"He must've been trying to get her to safety," said Mum.

Another helicopter departed, passing close enough to our position so that I could feel the downdraught from its rotors. That left just two more transports.

"We have to get you boys on to one of those 'copters," said Dad.

"He's right," said Zack. "All of you, go now. You'll be safe." There was steel in his voice. "I'll make sure of it."

I sensed that he was about to go off and do something brave and stupid. I grabbed his arm. "You never played the game," I said, my voice a desperate whisper. "You can't win. There isn't a superhero in the universe who can beat Gordon the World-Eater. You'll die."

Gently he prised off my fingers. "I'll be fine. Now, go."

With that, he stepped on to the parapet. I could almost hear the trumpeters strike up a fanfare as he prepared to leap into the fray. If he wouldn't listen to me, then maybe Mum or Dad could persuade him. Of course, I'd have to reveal his secret identity, but better that than the alternative.

They stood in a line across the roof – Mum, Dad, Serge and Josh – all in their superhero costumes: Peter Pan, Jor-El, Matter-Eater Lad and, uh, Shark Flutter.

I felt an idea stir. It swirled about, fired off a few synapses and then popped into the bit of the brain that recognises sheer brilliance.

"That's it! Za– Star Lad, wait!"

But it was too late, he had launched himself into the sky. My words were blown away by the powerful currents of wind that continued to rage in the wake of Gordon's latest cyclone attack. Behind me I could hear my parents yelling from the roof door, urging me to leave. I ignored them, trying to find some calm amid the sound and fury.

"I know how to defeat him," I sounded out in my head. "Zack? Can you hear me?"

Was Stellar still jamming all telepathic signals? Would my brother be able to pick up the crucial message?

Zack slowed and settled into a hover, his voice a grumble in my head. "I *knew* you'd do something like this. You always do," he complained.

"I do not." I cast my mind back to our previous encounters with Christopher Talbot and the sue-dunham invaders. "OK, so yes, maybe I do. But have I ever been wrong?"

"Not yet," he said grimly. "OK, so what's this brilliant pl—"

Before he could finish, a great hand wearing a spiked glove reached up from beneath like a shark for a dangling

153

swimmer and closed around him.

Gordon the World-Eater had materialised directly below Zack.

I could only watch in horror as he was carried off in the giant's fist. His legs kicked furiously and then went limp. I felt our telepathic bond snap.

"No-o-o!" My wail was lost in the whirlwind that followed. With a grotesque howl of victory, Gordon directed another blast of cyclone breath towards our little group on the comic shop. We were lifted off our feet and sent spinning high over the rooftops. I was dimly aware of the others caught in the updraught. We were rising fast, but soon we'd top out and then it was a one-way trip, straight down to our doom.

For a second I felt weightless. I'd reached the peak of my short flight.

The town centre lay far below. It all looked so peaceful and normal from up here.

The change of direction hit me like a hammer-blow, shattering my brief feeling of calm. I lost sight of the others as we tumbled uncontrollably to earth. We were seconds away from ending up as splodges on the High Street. As I fell, a phrase popped into my head; an expression that people in olden times used whenever they believed the world was ending, which was a lot, since in those days they thought the slightest thing signalled the apocalypse. Bad harvest? Eternal darkness. Tea leaves in the shape of a goat? Armageddon. Confusing prophecy in French? Judgment Day.

The phrase was: *The end is nigh.* I think "nigh" means "near". But as I plummeted out of the sky, the image of Gordon the World-Eater marching off with the lifeless Zack seared into my vision, I realised the end was way past nigh.

It was here.

The ground rose towards me, filling my vision.

I fell below the level of the library. Last half second. I flung my arms in front of my face in a futile protective gesture. I braced for impact.

And came to a sudden stop less than a metre above the street.

To my relief I saw that I wasn't the only one. Mum, Dad and Serge were similarly suspended, bodies held in mid-air like glitches in a videogame. Briefly I wondered what had become of Josh.

One thought burst through my surprise: only a telekinetic safety net could have arrested a fall like that. Zack must have freed himself from Gordon's clutches! With hope rising I felt myself gently lowered the final short distance to the ground.

"I still blame you."

I jerked my head up at the sound of that voice. Stellar stood before me. It was his telekinetic power that had caught me, not Zack's. All my hope vanished in an instant, replaced by blind fury.

"You!" I launched myself at him, knocking him to the ground.

Kneeling astride his chest I shook him by the shoulders. "You caused this. I wish you'd never come here. I hate you! I hate you! To the ends of the multiverse, I hate you!"

He could have brushed me off as easily as Gordon had swatted him, but instead he just lay there, taking his punishment.

"Hey, Luke, up here, mate!"

I lifted my head to see Josh Khan in his Shark Flutter costume. He was alive. More remarkably, he appeared to be flying. I rubbed my eyes and saw that he was held aloft by a bunch of flapping birds. At his side, controlling them, flew Lara. So Josh had got his wish to fly with Dark Flutter after all. His grin lit up an otherwise miserable day – at least it had turned out well for someone. Lara brought him in for a smooth landing.

"That. Was. Major! I mean, seriously awesome sauce," he gabbled. "Can we do it again?"

Everyone seemed to be in one piece. A little way off, Mum lay on the ground, too stunned to move, making moaning noises. Dad was on his hands and knees, repeating something about "terra firma" and kissing the pavement, which didn't look hygienic. Serge was on his feet, wandering around dazed.

Lara managed to peel Josh off her long enough to check on me. "That's the last time I complain about starlings," she said. "Luke, are you all right?"

"Yes," Stellar and I answered together. I glowered at him.

"Gordon the World-Eater took Zack," I said, my voice breaking. "He had no chance."

"There was nothing I could do," said Lara despondently.

"I'll try contacting him telepathically," said Stellar.

"You don't think I already tried?" I snapped. I'd been shouting his name in my head ever since he was snatched. "He's not responding."

"You don't think—" began Lara.

"No," insisted Stellar, leaping to his feet. "He's alive. We'll save him."

"*We* can't save anyone," I said.

"You're not making sense," said Lara. "If not us, then who? There isn't anyone else."

"What are you proposing?" asked Serge.

It was our last shot. The last shot anyone in the world would take. I took a deep breath.

"The ultimate crossover."

18
NICE SUIT

Other Luke didn't have much going for him in the superpowers department, but I had to admit that he could devise a pretty good plan under some quite stressful conditions.

Another helicopter departed, laden down with frightened civilians. That left just one more.

"The whole plan hinges on you, Stellar," said Luke once he had talked me through the details.

"Good," I said. "You couldn't ask for a more amazing, um … hinge."

"Yeah, but I'm sure you'll understand if it doesn't fill the rest of us with great enthusiasm."

I was going to object, but I could see his point. After all, I had brought Gordon the World-Eater here in the first place. Even though I still blamed Other Luke for goading me.

"Can we trust you?" asked Lara.

Before I could answer, Other Luke cut in. "We have no other choice." He laid a hand on my shoulder. "Keep your telepathic line open. I'll coordinate from the ground."

"Got it."

"So what are you waiting for? GO!"

I took to the sky, climbing straight up on full power. I glanced to one side to see Dark Flutter keeping pace with me thanks to a gaggle of geese, their powerful wings beating the air. She fixed me with a look of deep suspicion. We levelled out after a hundred metres for a view of the battlefield.

The horizon was alight with superpowers. Gordon the World-Eater's devastating attacks were answered by tracer fire from ground and air forces, but it was no use. Burning, trampling and lasering, he laid waste to everything in his path. I could see no sign of Zack and my Stellar Scanner wasn't picking up his signal, but I wouldn't allow myself to fear the worst. It couldn't be happening. Not now.

"S.C.A.R.F. leader to Stellar. Have you a visual on

target? Over." Other Luke's voice sounded loud and clear in my head.

"Strangers in the night, exchanging glances, wondering in the night what were the chances, we'd be sharing lo-o-ove..." sang Serge.

"I'm starving. I could really go for a McDonald's right now." And that was Josh.

The problem with leaving your telepathic superpower wide open was that you picked up everyone's thoughts, all of the time.

I broadcast my feelings on the subject. "Enough chat, people. Let's concentrate on the world-eating terror, shall we?"

With my thoughts clear I proceeded to carry out the first part of Other Luke's plan. Focusing on a patch of empty sky above the comic shop, I formed a picture in my head and declared, "I am opening the primary gerbil-hole."

It appeared instantly, a dark splotch in the light of day. From there it began to grow, swirling like cosmic chocolate and vanilla ice-cream ripple. Somewhere in the far reaches of the multiverse, I felt something stir.

"Is it working?" Lara shouted over the flapping of geese.

"It better be."

Across on the other side of town, Gordon the World-Eater continued his rampage. So far he hadn't spotted

161

what I was up to, but I couldn't count on it remaining that way for long. I created the next three holes in quick succession and crossed my fingers. For a second or two nothing happened, but then they began to take on the distinctive shape of figures. Four human-shaped holes reached across the afternoon sky like paper-chain people.

"They're coming." It was Serge's excited voice in my head. "They're coming!"

Other Luke's plan had relied on the answer to one question: when Zorbon picked me to become Stellar in my world, and Zack to be Star Lad here, what happened in all the other worlds?

"On every Earth, in every tree house that night, a hero was chosen," Other Luke had explained. "There isn't a single superhero in the universe who can defeat Gordon the World-Eater, but together maybe, just maybe, *they* can."

Four masked figures blasted out of the gerbil-holes, capes streaming behind them.

Four superheroes recruited from their universes for the greatest team-up ever.

"Is that *moi*?" Serge's voice rang in my head.

It was indeed. A different version of him, one who through a combination of events I could only guess at, had been granted superpowers.

Star-Serge, for want of a better name, wore his costume with *panache* (which was a French word that meant being elegant without really trying). When you see a superhero fly it's always an impressive sight, but until I clapped eyes on him I never imagined anyone could soar with so much style. Star-Serge's beautifully cut costume was in a subtle grey, suggesting it belonged to the sort of hero who didn't need to shout about his abilities. Most capes fluttered or flapped. His *murmured*. At the centre of his chest shone his sigil, a silver three-pronged spear. At first I took it to be a trident like Aquaman's, but as he came closer I saw that it was actually a dinner fork.

The next member of the elite group sported a pair of stubby wings and a dorsal fin on which his cape kept snagging.

"Shark Flutter," yelled Josh in my head, ignoring my order to keep a lid on useless chatter. "It's me! No way. I'm a superhero too. Hey, Luke-*ster*, you seeing this! I'm. A. Superhero. Woo-hoo!"

"Not aerodynamically possible," grumbled Other Luke.

Beside me I heard Lara gasp at the approach of the third hero. "You have got to be kidding."

Flying towards us was her big sister, Cara. I mean, it was Cara from an alternate dimension, but it was her all right. A lot of superheroes are simple to understand, primary coloured right down to their feelings. But you could tell just by looking that Cara was *complex*. I bet that it rained a lot in her universe and she spent a good deal of time staring from windows with regret. She wore a dark-blue and gold costume that included a cape, skirt and high boots, and a Wonder Woman-style metal headband etched with a cluster of stars.

Star-Cara – Stara? – hovered in front of Lara and folded her arms. She cast an inquisitive eye over her little sister from another world, studying her from top to bottom.

"Are those my boots?"

"Your old ones," replied Lara, adding in a slightly whiney voice, "Mum said I could have them."

Cara was about to respond when Lara looked past her shoulder. "Uh, who's that?" she asked, clearly keen to change the subject.

I vaguely recognised the fourth superhero. "It's ... that kid. Y'know, the one who sits at the back in English."

"Nuh-uh," said Josh, still tuned in to my mind. "I think it's that kid in my German class – the one who's always got a runny nose."

"Are you certain?" said Non-Super Serge. "He resembles that boy who had the accident with the Van de Graaff generator in the physics lab."

In my head I heard Other Luke give a disapproving

snort.

"Situation report, S.C.A.R.F. leader," I said. "What's up?"

"Nothing," he mumbled. "Well, I mean not *nothing*. I know we're facing Armageddon and everything, but honestly, you're telling me that all this lot get given superpowers and told to save their worlds, ahead of *me*. Even *that kid*? If I ever meet Zorbon, we're going to have words."

There wasn't time to listen to him complain. I addressed the new arrivals. Ideally, I'd have liked to call them by some cool superhero team name, but nothing came immediately to mind and there were more important things to focus on.

"OK, everyone," I began. "I used my awesome but mysterious new superpower to summon you from your universes for a reason. Now I shall lay out the mission for you."

Star-Serge waved a hand lazily in the direction of the chaos caused by Gordon the World-Eater. "An all-powerful supervillain threatens this world, so you bring assistance from alternate worlds. A classic crossover, *oui*?"

"Uh, yeah, that about covers it."

"*Bon*. Shall we begin?"

"Hold on," said Dark Flutter. "Before we go all Justice

Team here—"

"League," I interrupted. "It's Justice League."

"Whatever. I have a question. If Gordon the World-Eater is invincible, how can we defeat him?"

I was about to explain precisely how, but Josh aka Shark Flutter beat me to the Doomsday-sized punch.

"Happens all the time," he said. "All-powerful characters regularly get defeated. Apocalypse, Juggernaut, Darkseid, there are loads. Just because you're invincible doesn't mean you're unbeatable."

"Uh, that's exactly what it means," said Dark Flutter.

Shark Flutter shrugged. "Not in comics. Right, Luke?"

"Right," I said. Shark Flutter was looking at me oddly. "Something bothering you?"

"It's just weird seeing you with superpowers, Luke-meister. Quite a relief, to be honest. In my universe you missed out and you're really miffed about it. All. The. Time. Won't stop going on about it. My Luke's kind of a pain, actually."

It was a good job Other Luke couldn't hear what Shark Flutter thought about him.

"Excuse me?" said an indignant voice. I'd forgotten that my telepathic power was still on. "What does he think about me?"

Awkward. I pretended that there was static on the line.

"Sorry, S.C.A.R.F. leader, CRRK BZZZ. You're breaking FZZZ up."

"You don't get radio static on a telepathic connection. Oh, never mind. Just get on with it, Stellar."

Suddenly more voices entered my head. It was Mum and Dad. Seemed they had recovered enough from their fall to take in what was going on around them. I could see them far below, heading along the street to rejoin Other Luke.

"You wanted a personal appearance from a superhero – well, you got one," said Mum. "Actually, you got six."

"But how?" said Dad. "This is … they are … *impossible*."

Of course! He didn't know it, but Dad had landed on the thing I'd been rooting around for since the four superheroes shot from their gerbil-holes. I felt the faint stirrings of hope once more as the world's newest superhero team formed up in a delta pattern about me. Six supers. One mission. And a name.

"OK, Impossibles, let's save the world."

19
THE IMPOSSIBLES

The name was the last thing I heard over Stellar's telepathic connection before he shut down all communication to concentrate on the daunting task ahead. He had accomplished the first part of my plan by bringing the Impossibles to this universe. Now he put part two into action. Extending a hand he moulded a new gerbil-hole out of thin air and directed his power to expand it. The single spot lengthened and widened. In a few minutes it would be big enough for its purpose, but not yet. And until then, Stellar and the rest of the heroes had to hold off Gordon the World-Eater.

The High Street blazed with a firestorm of shrink rays,

heat rays, cyclone breath, energy beams and more, as he unleashed every power my six-year-old self had granted him.

"Luke, come on." It was Mum. "Boys, we're leaving. Right now!"

Before I could object, she and Dad herded me, Serge and Josh along the street towards the last evacuation helicopter.

Above us, the Impossibles ducked and looped, threw up force fields, deflected lightning bolts and sonic blasts, but though they confounded each fresh attack, Gordon the World-Eater always seemed to have one more to hurl at them.

Star-Serge drew out his asthma inhaler but instead of taking a puff, aimed it at Gordon and squeezed the top, releasing some kind of enveloping gas cloud. Gordon simply inhaled the cloud and a moment later discharged a cosmic burp.

The helicopter sat ready to depart, rotor-blades spinning, hold groaning with passengers. More scrambled aboard through open doors on both sides of the aircraft. At each entrance, airmen helped those they could. Dad lifted me up and I was gathered inside. Josh and Serge followed. Pressed into the crowded compartment, I made a decision. My brother was out there somewhere. He needed me, whether he liked it or not. I had to get off that helicopter.

Mum and Dad were among the last of the evacuees. As soon as they were in, the airman on that side closed the door. It locked with a resounding clang. The door on the other side of the aircraft was already sliding shut. I wriggled through the crush of bodies, squeezed through the narrowing gap and slid down to the ground. In the confusion of the evacuation I'd made it out without my parents noticing.

There was a blast of noise and dust as the helicopter took off.

"*Attends*, wait for me," said a voice from behind.

"Serge?" He'd followed me out. And he wasn't alone.

"OK, Luke-*meister*," said Josh, rubbing his hands together. "What's the plan?"

Before I could answer, a downdraught blew us off our feet. Hurled across the street, I smacked against the side of a bus stop and slid to the ground. I lifted my spinning head to see the sole of Gordon's massive sandal descending at attack speed. Just before I was turned into pavement chewing gum, That Kid swooped in and threw up a force field. The sandal bounced off the invisible barrier, the brute strength of the attack cracking open the road. In the breach, a broken water main spurted, severed electrical cables sparked.

The brooding figure of Star Cara put herself between us and the monstrous Gordon and placed her hands either side of her headband. The collection of stars glowed like supernovae and a second later ejected some kind of starburst. It struck Gordon on the shoulder.

He shrugged off the blast, planted his feet and responded with a magnetic beam attack that wrenched off Cara's headband, removing the power from her arsenal.

Without pausing he dispatched a cluster attack of his own at Shark Flutter, raining down balls of glowing lava. Shark Flutter twisted and turned, but couldn't evade all of them. A fiery chunk caught him. He spun out of control and for a moment it looked like he'd been neutralised. He tumbled from sight, below the level of the buildings, and I held my breath along with the others. A second later he soared up again, held aloft by Dark Flutter and her birds.

"The *gerbille-*'ole, it must be big enough now," said Serge.

The hole was a gaping wound in the sky, a hundred-metre-high rip in reality.

Stellar had made the same calculation. His cape whipping behind him, he marshalled the other superheroes to form a semicircle around Gordon the World-Eater. In position, they focused their telekinetic powers like a lens on a single point. I can never remember if it's convex or concave, but it was one of them.

This was the final part of my plan. It had to work.

"Do it," I muttered. "FIRE!"

The Impossibles unleashed the power of five universes.

Unlike laser-beams and fire-breath, telekinesis was usually invisible. However, the force of their combined effort warped the air into a kaleidoscopic beam that struck the World-Eater full in his star-filled face.

He stumbled, driven back towards the yawning hole. In that moment I could tell that he understood what I intended for him, but too late. A howl of hate spilled from his mouthless void.

"That's it," I hissed. "Send that thing back where it came from."

The gerbil-hole opened behind him like the maw of a much bigger fish. The Impossibles pushed. The gravity of the gerbil-hole pulled. There was no way back.

"It is working!" yelled Serge.

But he had spoken too soon.

Raising each of his sandalled feet in turn, Gordon the World-Eater dug in his massive heels. And played yet another card.

He started to grow. In seconds he was twice his original size, and then he doubled again, so tall now that he pierced the clouds. A hundred times more powerful than before, he inched his way out of the gerbil-hole's grip, back towards the Impossibles.

"*Non!*" cried Serge, clasping a hand to his mouth.

"He's too strong," said Josh.

With horror I realised I had been wrong about his name from the start. Gordon really was now big enough to eat the world.

And then it happened.

Above us, the thunderclap of the sound barrier yielding to powers beyond understanding.

A glowing streak in the sky.

Serge shielded his eyes against the intensity of the light that spilled from what we now saw to be a speeding figure. "He is alive!"

Soaring over our heads, cape rippling like a knight's banner, eyes locked on his destiny…

Star Lad joined the fight.

Now the Impossibles were seven. A much better number for a superhero team than six, in my opinion. He took his place beside Stellar in the semicircle.

It was time. Or the end of time, if the next few seconds went the wrong way.

173

"One more push, *mon ami*," Serge muttered grimly. "You can do it."

The universe can't hold its breath, of course, but if it could then in that moment I'm sure every raging supernova, every noisy gravity wave, every fizzing sun from here to eternity would have fallen silent.

There was a gathering pause, into which Star Lad and the others poured the combined might of their telekinetic powers.

They lashed Gordon the World-Eater with an impossible amount of energy.

He stumbled and dropped to one knee. We felt the shockwave of his impact roll over us.

Somehow he hung on.

The Impossibles were at maximum power. It flashed through my mind that they had no more to give. Clearly, that thought hadn't occurred to my brother.

Like everyone else in the world I'd watched the satellite feed of Zack knocking out Nemesis. I was with him aboard the sue-dunham mothership when he took on the invaders, but back then he'd been weakened by alien flu. So this was the first time I'd seen him, in person…

Go. Full. Star. Lad.

My brother leapt from the circle of superheroes and in the blink of an eye accelerated to maximum speed. He was a blur as he struck Gordon the World-Eater full-force in the chest. The monster staggered backwards. And this time he couldn't stop himself.

He toppled back into the hole.

There was a noise like ten thousand people sucking the last of a thick milkshake through a straw, and the dark boundary between worlds sealed itself up. Green auroras of light licked at the edges of the fading tear and then vanished. In the late afternoon sky all that remained of the epic confrontation were palls of smoke rising from the devastated High Street and a bunch of exhausted superheroes.

Gordon the World-Eater was no more.

20
LUKE BEFORE YOU LEAP

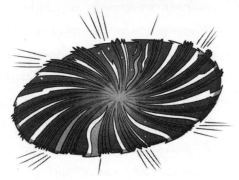

After the noise and chaos came the hush, the only sounds the breeze in the bare branches of the trees that lined the street and the distant thump of rotor-blades. For one terrible moment I thought Zack had gone through the gerbil-hole with Gordon. But then a cloud slid past and he emerged from behind it, a slight figure floating in the unexpected quiet of what had turned out to be a very strange Saturday afternoon.

Zack's voice whispered in my head. It was weak, thready. His telepathic power faded in and out.

"Next time," he said, "how about a nice game of Boggle? I reckon even you can't turn Boggle into a multidimensional apocalyptic menace."

"How often do I have to say it – this wasn't my fault," I complained. But right then I really didn't care. And whatever I'd once thought of Stellar, I couldn't deny that he had come through in the end. For that he had earned my grudging respect. OK, yes, he could've been a bit more careful about nearly causing the end of the world in the first place, but we've all been there.

Star Lad wasn't moving. He hung there in the blue, like a swimmer far out at sea exhausted by the current. The fight had utterly drained him. He'd need hours exposed to starlight to recover his strength. And as I wondered how he was keeping himself up, suddenly he wasn't.

Nearby, in the same patch of sky, Stellar shot out a hand and used what remained of his own powers to catch the falling Zack and guide him gently down on to the roof of the comic shop. As soon as my brother touched down, I began to make my way the short distance back to meet him.

"What is he doing now?" asked Serge.

Stellar dotted the sky with four new gerbil-holes. As soon as the first one appeared, he waved a hand and launched That Kid through it.

"I think he's sending the Impossibles back to their

worlds," I said.

Shark Flutter went next, yanked unceremoniously back to his universe.

"Not fair," objected Josh. "I wanted to meet myself and tell me what an excellent job I did."

Stellar seemed to be in a hurry. He dispatched the remaining superheroes as if he was trying to catch the last post. If I hadn't just watched them team up and save the world, I'd have said he didn't want them around. But why, after all they'd done? Unless...

"Oh no." I had a terrible premonition.

"What is wrong?" asked Serge.

Even though we'd just defeated an invincible megademon, I had a horrible feeling that something worse was about to happen.

"The Impossibles were the only ones who could stop him," I said.

I picked up the pace. Now I was in a race with my Evil Twin. Stellar's plan to lure Zack to his world had failed spectacularly, but he wasn't finished yet.

The three of us reached the comic shop. Inside was a wreck. Shelves were overturned, comics trampled by fleeing customers, but I barely noticed the mess as I made a dash for the stairs. Serge and Josh were a little way behind, but I couldn't wait.

I stumbled through the roof door, banging it open. Stellar stood with his back to me. Alerted by my not exactly stealthy arrival, he turned round. He held Zack's limp body in his arms.

"Luke, be careful!" The cry came from above. Lara dangled high over the roof, as immobile as a pinned butterfly. She must have figured things out too, and Stellar was using his powers to keep her at bay. She fought against the telekinetic bonds, but it was useless. He was too strong for her.

Behind me I heard footsteps. It was Josh and Serge. With a nod of his head, Stellar used the same power to swing the door shut in their faces. He held it there, barring them from the roof.

Now it was just me and him.

I took a step closer. "Is Zack…?"

"Stay there, please," Stellar said in a warning tone. "Zack's fine, just exhausted. Don't worry, he's safe with me. I promise I won't let anything happen to him."

Over his shoulder I glimpsed an object shooting across the sky. For a second I thought it was a meteorite, but then it drew closer and Stellar plucked it out of the air using telekinesis. It was a metal cube painted blue and streaked with layers of a glass-like material. Some kind of desk ornament.

"What's that?" I asked.

"Call it a loose end," said Stellar. "And now it's time for us to leave."

"I won't let you take my brother," I said, although I had no idea how I was going to stop him. And we both knew it.

"Gerbils and rocket shoes were one thing, but until today I didn't know I could send *people* across universes. I came here in Zorbon's ship, but I don't need it any more."

He blinked. Behind him a gerbil-hole appeared, at first no bigger than a raisin, but in seconds it loomed above the comic shop like a gigantic cinnamon swirl. An accompanying tremor shook the foundations, sending clouds of dust and debris into the air.

He turned towards the portal.

"No. Wait." I was growing desperate. "What do you need Zack for?" I gestured to the devastated High Street. "I think we've pretty much established that there's no actual supervillain in your world for him to fight." Stellar remained silent. "Why would you even want him? He outshines us at everything, everyone likes him better than us. But most of all, why would you want *my* Zack when you've already got one of your own?"

Stellar studied me through the haze of dust. He seemed

to be making up his mind about something.

"You once asked me what it's like to be a superhero. There's a lot of talk about power and responsibility, but I didn't appreciate what that meant until it was too late. When Nemesis threatened my world, I was the only one who could stop it. I had all that power and I couldn't wait for the chance to prove myself. But..." His throat dried up and he choked out the next words. "I failed in my responsibility. I was hailed as a hero for saving the earth, but when I returned from space after diverting Nemesis, I found my home blasted to pieces by a stray chunk. It was a miracle that Mum and Dad survived. But Zack..." He looked down at the unconscious figure in his arms. "I saved my world, but I couldn't save him."

Zack was dead. Atomised by Nemesis.

I heard a weird buzzing in my ears and I felt sick. Life without Zack was unimaginable. No one eating the last of the good cereal *every time*, no one using up all the hot water so I had to have a cold shower, Mum and Dad not dismally comparing my school reports to Zack's. It would be a world without endless squabbles over pointless stuff. It would be awful. The sick feeling turned into stomach ache. Even just the thought of losing my brother physically hurt. The reality might drive me crazy. Stellar really had lost Zack. *His* Zack, I reminded myself. Mine was right here on this roof with me. Alive and…

I realised with stone-cold dread what Stellar was up to, why he had undertaken such a hazardous journey to my world. At first I'd assumed he wanted to replace me. I couldn't have been more wrong.

He was replacing his brother with mine.

"I never got the chance to say goodbye," said Stellar quietly. "This is yours."

I couldn't – wouldn't – say it. All that came out of my mouth was, "Don't!"

I stretched out a hand. A futile gesture. Maybe I was hoping that I'd suddenly acquired superpowers. That in this, my moment of need, some last-page-of-the-comic-twist would prevent evil triumphing over good. Instead, I could only watch as Stellar stepped off the parapet and flew him and Zack towards the churning hole. I heard myself let out a cry, which was swallowed in the tumult of the whirling portal.

Two figures star-bright against the darkness. Zack raised his head. Confused and stunned, he met my gaze just for a second. And then he was gone.

The gerbil-hole was already shrinking. In a second or two it would vanish. But Stellar had forgotten one thing. We were the same person. He'd risked everything for his brother.

Now it was my turn.

I backed up as far as I dared, rocked on my heel and took a running jump. I felt my knee buckle under me as I launched myself off the roof. Uh-oh. The gap between the comic shop and the hole was a lot wider than I'd anticipated. I wasn't going to make it. But it was too late. Out of the corner of my eye I glimpsed Serge and Josh on the roof. I could tell that they were yelling at me, but all I could hear was my own terrified breathing.

And then not even that.

21
LUKE ME UP WHEN YOU'RE IN TOWN

I crashed down on top of the bins in the alley behind the comic shop. Slithering down to the ground, I checked myself for damage. Surprisingly, I was in one piece, but that was the only good news. Stellar had spirited Zack away to his universe, while I was stuck here. I'd failed. Picking myself up I hobbled round to the front of the shop. Perhaps all was not lost. I'd regroup with S.C.A.R.F. and we'd make a new plan.

The smell of chips lingered. A customer exited the shop carrying a paper bag emblazoned with a logo I didn't recognise. As he passed me the same aroma wafted from the bag. When he had crossed my path, I saw past him.

What should have been Dad's comic shop was now some kind of fast-food restaurant.

Slowly I lifted my eyes to the shop front. Dad's new sign had gone and in its place hung an unfamiliar name.

"Chicken & Pickle?"

In the space of a heartbeat I knew.

This wasn't my world.

I'd made it. I was here, on Another Earth. My head spun faster than The Flash's legs. Dazed, I stumbled into the road, ignoring the angry hoot of car horns. I didn't care. All I knew was that I had to find Zack. I stood there, not knowing which way to turn. I had no idea where to start looking. Frustration welled inside me.

This wasn't helping me or Zack. I had to pull myself together. Closing my eyes, I attempted to contact him.

"Something something where am I?"

It was his voice! Zack was here.

"Something something look out he's got an ocelot!"

It might not have been "ocelot". Honestly, it was kind of hard to make out what he was thinking. And no matter how hard I tried, I couldn't make him hear me. It wasn't like before when Stellar jammed the signal. This was different, as if someone had draped a thick blanket over Zack's thoughts.

Not a blanket – a *force field*. If my hunch was correct, then Stellar was holding Zack a prisoner in the tree house, just as he had me.

There was the rattle of a diesel engine and the hiss of air-brakes as the 227 bus paused at its usual stop outside the comic shop. The 227 would take me home, and that's where I'd find Zack. I jumped on board. Thankfully, my bus pass worked in this dimension. I settled myself into a seat by the window as the bus pulled away.

Last month I'd travelled into space aboard an alien mothership, but now here I was in a different universe. To be honest, it was a bit disappointing – there were no futuristic floating cities or people commuting by hover-car. It was basically Bromley. But then, like the comic shop, when I looked closer I could tell that I was somewhere else. Advertising hoardings displayed posters for films I'd never heard of, except for the latest *Star Wars*. I felt reassured to know that *Star Wars* remained a constant in all universes. However, here the yellow of McDonald's arches was a slightly different shade. And stripy jumpers were seriously in fashion.

I was a stranger in a familiar land.

There were larger differences too. We stopped outside the library – or what used to be the library. It had gone. Not that it had been closed because of cuts or anything like that. It had been razed to the ground; all that remained was a deep crater. From my elevated seat on the bus I could see over a temporary fence plastered with "Danger, Keep Out" signs, which cordoned off the great scar.

The bus set off again, rumbling along its route out to the suburbs. We passed a terrace of white-painted houses with several missing, like a row of disfigured teeth. Where houses had once stood now lay only rubble. It was obvious to me what had caused the destruction.

Nemesis.

In my world Star Lad had stopped the killer asteroid in its tracks, allowing just a few small chunks of space rock to make it past him and collide with Earth. Stellar had been less successful in protecting his Earth.

It was raining by the time the bus pulled up at my stop. I jumped off and hurried the short distance to Moore Street. Stellar and I may have chosen different paths, but we still lived on the same street. Packs of stray dogs and cats roamed like rival gangs, weeds grew unchecked through cracks in the unmended pavement. It felt as if civilisation was hanging on, but only just.

I passed Lara and Cara's house, glimpsing Lara through the upstairs window of her bedroom. Lowering my head, I walked quickly on. I didn't want her to see me, since my presence would raise too many awkward questions.

My trainers slapped against the rain-slick pavement as I came to a stop outside my house at 128 Moore Street. Except, it wasn't. Just like the library, it had gone. Where it once stood was a fence with a sign that read: "Danger – Keep Out." Stellar had told me that the house was obliterated by Nemesis but seeing it in person was quite another thing. Shaken, I leaned against the gatepost to steady myself. The metal post came away in my hand. I wondered how Stellar must have felt in my world, seeing his home in one piece, just as it used to be in his.

I heard his terrible words again. Zack was dead. Gone. He wasn't my brother, I kept reminding myself. Not my house. Not my brother. He was the Other One – the other Zack. They shared a name, a childhood, but not a universe. I clung to the thought that the last time I'd seen my Zack he was still very much alive. So what was this great lump in my throat? Why was I trying really hard not to cry?

One time when we were little, Zack was rushed to hospital with what turned out to be a broken leg. In all the commotion, I was forgotten and no one took the time to explain to me exactly what was going on. I could remember standing in Accident & Emergency, gagging on the smell of disinfectant. I'd watched as they wheeled him through a set of swing doors, and then I'd begun to sob uncontrollably because I thought it was the last time I'd ever see him. That's how I felt standing there in the rain.

"Come on, Luke," I urged myself. "Keep it together. Stay on target."

I squeezed through the gap in the fence. I circled the rim of a shallow crater filled with rubble and bricks and bits of what I recognised as our former kitchen. Incredibly, one wall still stood. Halfway up it hung a shelf that I remembered Dad putting up. Most of his DIY didn't last a week, but this one had survived a direct asteroid strike. I pushed a toe through the rubble, turning over a blackened object lying on the ground. It was my Green Lantern alarm clock, burnt almost beyond recognition.

In the wreckage of the back garden stood the solitary oak tree, and cradled in its protective branches was my tree house. One end sat lower than the other, presumably dislodged when the asteroid hit, but other than that it seemed intact. It also looked uninhabited. Bending down, I picked up half a house brick. If Stellar's force field were in place, then a well-aimed projectile would bounce off the invisible barrier. I pulled back my arm and hurled the brick. There was a dull thud as it smacked against the tree house and dropped straight down. No force field. Which meant no Zack. So where was he? I was back to square one.

"Luke?"

I whirled round to see Lara emerging from the gap in the fence.

"I thought it was you," she said, picking her way across the uneven ground. She flicked open an umbrella and studied me from beneath it. "I saw you from my window."

She looked like my Lara, but I reminded myself that she wasn't the same person. I had to be careful. It would be all too easy to give myself away by saying the wrong thing.

"How was Devon?" she asked.

"Devon?"

"Y'know, the multi-activity residential adventure centre?"

Stellar's cover story. Of course. "Oh, it was great," I lied. "We did abseiling, kayaking, uh…" What else did people do at those things? "Bull-riding."

"Bull-riding?" She tilted her head and considered me through curious eyes. "You seem different."

Uh-oh. She was on to me and I'd barely opened my mouth. "Well, after all that running about and climbing stuff my self-esteem is up here now," I said, raising a hand above my head.

"No, that's not it."

"I've had my hair cut," I lied.

"No you haven't," she said, walking round me, inspecting me from every angle. "It's just as awful as it's always been."

"What's wrong with my hair?" I knew it wasn't important, but I couldn't help ask.

She snorted. "Well, a wash wouldn't do it any harm for a start. What is it with boys and soap?"

A small furry shape scurried out from beneath one of our old kitchen cabinets and ran between us.

"*Ugh*, a rat," said Lara, jumping back, the umbrella spinning in her hand. She shivered in horror. "Disgusting things. This place has been overrun with them since N-Day."

"End Day?"

She shot me a confused look.

N-Day. I realised too late that's what she'd said. Nemesis Day, of course. We'd marked it in our world with a holiday and a made-for-TV movie, but something about the name suggested theirs had been a darker day than ours. Briefly I wondered if that's how little kids in this world learned their alphabet. A is for Apple, B is for

Book ... N was for Nemesis.

There was a series of squeaks and the first rat was joined by a friend. They sat in full view, picnicking on scraps. They were taking a risk being here with all those cats wandering the street.

"Couldn't you just ask them to move somewhere else?" I suggested.

"What are you talking about?"

"Use your superpowers, of course."

"Oh ha-ha, very funny. The only person round here with superpowers is Stellar. And I don't see him anywhere, do you?"

She was serious.

The earth rotates at 1700 kilometres an hour, and when Lara said those words I felt every dizzying spin. It meant that in this world she wasn't Dark Flutter *and* she didn't know about Stellar. I was dumbfounded. Lara Lee had no idea that her neighbour, Luke Parker, was a superhero.

It struck me then just how different this world was from my own. I'd hoped that I could operate here as normal, but normal was playing a kazoo and wearing a fish for a hat. I was adrift, on my own without S.C.A.R.F. If my mission were to succeed, then I needed help. I had to take drastic action.

"You're right," I said. "I haven't had my hair cut, but I am different. I'm not the Luke you know. I'm an almost identical version from another universe."

She sighed and began to walk away. "See you at school, Luke."

Naturally, she didn't believe me. I had to convince her, but how?

"Lara, wait. I can prove it."

She paused. I could tell from the set of her shoulders that she was considering my outrageous statement. I held up my Lara's phone. With a fleeting pang of guilt about roaming charges, I switched it on. "It's yours. I mean it belongs to the version of Lara who lives in my universe."

"Ooh, so Other Me has a smartphone?"

"Yes, you got it when—" I fumbled. "Never mind. In here is all the proof you could ever want. But—"

"No kidding. There's a 'but'?"

"It's locked and I don't know the passcode." I offered out the handset. "Humour me."

Reluctantly, she retraced her footsteps and with a bored flick of the wrist laid a finger on the fingerprint scanner. The phone unlocked and the Home screen appeared.

"OK, fine." She crossed her arms. "But now I'm

thinking 'clever hack', rather than 'evidence of parallel worlds'."

It took me a few seconds to find what I was searching for. I turned the screen to her. On it was the photo my Lara had taken in the tree house during Stellar's welcome party, featuring her, Zack, Serge, Luke ... and Luke.

Intrigued, Parallel Lara leaned in to scrutinise the picture.

"You knew as soon as you laid eyes on me that I'm not your Luke. Search your feelings. You know it to be true."

I could tell she was wavering.

She straightened. "For argument's sake, let's say this isn't some deeply astounding bit of Photoshop, and that I do believe you. In which case I have a question. Check that. I have *many* questions. But this one will do for starters."

"Shoot."

She extended a finger towards the photo. "Why am I wearing a superhero costume?"

22
LUKE DARKER

My brother is a superhero ... and so am I. My name is Luke Parker, I live in a mild-mannered part of London with my mum, dad and big brother Zack. OK, not yet. It would be a few days until I could reintroduce him, but soon Zack would be part of the family again.

In the meantime, he was safely out of sight in a location as secure as Gamma Base (which was designed to hold the Hulk). Chislehurst Caves were a local tourist attraction – more than twenty miles of twisting tunnels built under the countryside, with the main entrance little more than a mile from the High Street. According to legend, they were first dug out almost four thousand years ago by Druids who used them to perform human sacrifices, offering up the blood of their victims to the sun god. The atmosphere was an odd mix of foreboding and suburban – sort of ancient horrific rites with convenient access to Boots.

I ignored the main entrance, instead making my way through the car park and around the back of the café. In the middle of a clump of trees was a small rocky opening formed of two slabs, mossy and shaded, just far enough out of the way to be overlooked by most people. When I was younger, I'd briefly established a Batcave here, but gave up on the idea pretty quickly. It turns out that an underground Batcave is not an ideal HQ when you're claustrophobic and quite scared of the dark. However, I was older and less easily spooked these days.

I switched on my LED lantern and plunged inside. Deep within the cave system, following a route known only to me, I found Zack in a large cavern. He was asleep, his back resting against a rough stone wall, legs stretched out on a blanket I'd thrown over the uneven floor. I studied his face by the lantern-light. The battle with Gordon the World-Eater had left his powers depleted, which suited me fine for now. A fully charged Star Lad would pose a question I wasn't sure I had an answer for. I daren't let him regain full strength until I'd convinced him that his new life was here. In my world.

He looked peaceful and he needed to rest, so I felt bad about waking him, but there were things we had to discuss. I rocked his shoulder.

He stirred, sat up and rubbed his eyes. "Where am I?"

"You're home." I opened a packet of glow-sticks and scattered a few of them for extra illumination.

He cast a suspicious look around the place. "This doesn't look like my home."

"Well, no, I couldn't exactly rock up to Mum and Dad with you in tow. Not yet."

"I'm in *your* world?"

"It's your world now, Zack."

I could see him absorb this new information and dismiss it. He mashed his lips together. "I'm thirsty."

I reached into my backpack and pulled out a bottle of water. He gulped it down and when he'd drained the last drop he held the empty bottle, twisting and untwisting the cap.

"Luke was right – there never was a supervillain threatening your world." His voice was a mixture of surprise and disappointment. "You tried to lure me here under false pretences."

"I knew you wouldn't have come if I told you the truth."

"And what's that then?"

I told him.

It was hard explaining that in this world he had been killed by Nemesis, and it was all my fault. His initial shock turned to anger, but I'd been prepared for that. Boy, was he angry. I'd only ever seen him this furious once before, and that was years ago when I'd used his prize-winning English essay to line my pet gerbil's cage.

"Take me back to my world, right now," he ordered when I'd finished my story.

That wasn't an option. "Here's a magazine and some sandwiches." I handed him the magazine and a packet of cheese and onion on wholemeal.

"*Model Train Enthusiast Monthly*? Uh, I don't think so." He pressed it back into my hands.

"But you love trains. Ever since that trip we took to York to see the Flying Scotsman."

"Never been," he said. "We were meant to go, but then I got tonsillitis."

"Oh."

"And I don't like cheese and onion sandwiches either."

"But they're your favourite."

"Used to be, but I had a bad experience with some railway catering. Another reason why I'm not keen on trains." He shoved the sandwiches back at me. "We're not the same person."

"Yes you are," I snapped. Maybe it came out a bit

harsh. "You're identical. Quantum physics says so." I'd expected some resistance, but Zack was even more unwilling to accept his new reality than I'd anticipated. I had to sweeten the deal. "You never wanted to be a superhero, did you?"

Zack was silent, which I took as an invitation to elaborate.

"Here, in this world, you don't have to be. Forget about all that flying around and saving-people stuff. I'll do that. You can just be *you*."

As Star Lad he was unappreciated and tied down with red tape; the daily effort of concealing his identity exhausted him. I knew he'd had enough. What I offered was a release from that responsibility. I could tell he was thinking about it.

"I can't stay here," he said at last. "I have a life ... my family. At home."

"But we're here. We're all here, Zack."

"It's not the same. You're not—"

"*I am*. I'm your brother. I'm Luke." I gazed down at him. "Please don't leave me again." I could see that my words carried the same force as any superpower. His confused, angry expression melted away in front of my eyes.

"Get out," he said quietly, turning his back on me.

I set the magazine and sandwiches down beside

him. "In case you change your mind." I picked up the lantern. Ducking under the low stone arch that formed the exit, I paused. "Don't get any ideas about escaping. Your powers are too weak, and even if you did somehow manage to break through my force field, you'll never find your way out of here."

Zack didn't respond, just sat staring into space. I made my way out through a maze of tunnels, using my telekinetic power to smooth over my footprints, leaving no trace of my passing and offering no clue to anyone who happened to stumble across the entrance. I hid the lantern in an alcove and walked out into the quiet stillness of the scrubby wood. My encounter with Zack hadn't gone as well as I'd hoped and I needed to clear my head. I decided to take the long route home.

Via the Alps.

I flew at supersonic speeds through mountain passes, breathing in the cold, pure air. I performed a barrel-roll over Mont Blanc, scared the crampons out of a couple of mountaineers, and churned up a pretty spectacular wave on Lake Geneva. The important thing was that Zack was back. It was only natural that he would complain to begin with. There was no way back to his world – I'd made sure of that – so when he appreciated that he was here to stay, I felt sure he'd make the best of his situation. That was

Zack. Always making the best of things. It wouldn't be long before he was happy again.

I'd cheered myself up. I hadn't felt like this in ages. I'd rewritten the past, now the future was mine. *All mine.*

OK, admittedly, that did sound a bit Evil Twin-*ish*.

But I wasn't the bad guy. I'd saved the world – my world, anyway. Millions of people owed their lives to me. So what if I'd nicked one fourteen-year-old boy from a neighbouring universe. *One.* Could that really be called the act of a supervillain? Hardly. And if you were to take a poll of all the people I'd saved from Nemesis, all the families I'd kept alive, I bet they'd agree with me.

I arrived home in time for dinner. Pausing in my bedroom to hang up my costume, I glanced at my new Green Lantern alarm clock.

Other Luke would be sitting down to dinner in his universe too. I felt an unexpected jab of guilt, but shrugged it off and went downstairs to join the rest of my family.

Zack's place at the table was empty, just as it had been since it happened. But thanks to me, that was about to change. I'd spent ages working out the practicalities of reintroducing him. Mind control had been my first option. I'd decided to wipe people's minds and alter their memories of what happened. It would be as if Zack never died. One problem. I didn't have mind control powers. And then it struck me, why was I bothering with complicated plans when there was a much simpler way to achieve the same outcome? No trace of Zack had ever been found. I'd just say there had been a terrible mistake – that he wasn't killed by Nemesis. The asteroid strike caused amnesia and he'd wandered off. Now, at last, he'd found his way home. Mum and Dad were sure to accept him as their son. After all, he *was* their Zack, in almost every way – trains and sandwich fillings excepted. Of course, there was the issue of his superpowers. That was different. However, I was betting that he'd be perfectly happy to keep them under wraps and let me do all the superhero-ing in future.

"I thought you and I were working on the bird feeder after school today," said Dad. "Where've you been?"

"Flying over the Alps," I replied. "Everyone goes on about the Matterhorn, but really you should see the Grossglockner at sunset. Lovely peak."

With a weary sigh Dad assumed I was joking and passed me the potatoes.

I almost dropped the bowl.

"Luke! Be careful, son."

I wasn't listening. I'd just had an awful thought. When I left Zack, had I remembered to switch on the force field? He was almost certainly too weak to escape, but I couldn't take the risk. It was OK. I could activate it from here. I concentrated hard, sending my massive power out into the world, snaking through the suburbs to Zack's hiding place. I could feel my jaw clench and beads of sweat trickle down my forehead. Force field, force field, force f—

"Luke?" Mum interrupted my superpower-ing. She lowered her voice. "Do you need to go to the toilet?"

"No, I don't need the toilet," I snapped.

"It did look like you needed to go," agreed Dad, heaping his plate with salad. He passed me the bowl. "Roughage."

After dinner I went up to my room to do my homework. Not even superpowers can get you out of coordinating and subordinating conjunctions. I kicked off my shoes and lay down on my bed. Homework could wait. Now was the time to celebrate and I knew just how to reward myself for my success. I'd read every comic in the known universe, but that was OK. There were plenty more universes.

In my mind I pictured what I wanted. It wasn't long before the smell of chips filled the air and my bedroom began to shake. My sock drawer juddered out of its slot and crashed to the floor. Plaster dust rained down as a crack drew itself across the ceiling. Finally, a shimmering rectangle opened above my bed.

A comic fluttered from the hole and landed with a slap on the floor. I swept it up, the cover confirming what I'd hoped for, and expected.

"Batman versus Darth Vader." The impossible crossover. Not some fan-made mock-up, this had the smell, the feel, the official logos of a licensed story. Somewhere in the infinite multiverse this comic existed and I had brought it to me just by thinking about it. How cool was that?!

Other Luke could fret all he liked about my meddling with cosmic forces, I wasn't worried. I figured it was a bit like that time Dad went on a diet and I caught him in his shed, elbow-deep in a can of Sour Cream & Onion Pringles. He'd said two things. The first was, "Don't tell your mum." And then he'd added, "One more little crisp isn't going to make a difference, is it?" Well, on that basis, one more little hole in the universe couldn't make that much of a difference either. Could it?

Pushing the thought to the back of my mind, I settled down to discover who would win in this, the most longed-for contest: the Caped Crusader or the Dark Lord of the Sith? As I turned to the first page I reflected on what I'd achieved. Zack was back for good. Soon Mum and Dad would be happy again.

And we'd all live happily ever after.

23
BE ON THE LUKE OUT

"I have eyes on the target," said Lara. The two of us were hiding in a bush outside Stellar's house, watching him through a lighted window. "He is sitting down to dinner. He is using his fork to spear a piece of sausage. Now he is lifting the fork with the sausage to his mouth. Now he is eating the sausage—"

"OK, OK, I get it," I cut her off. "When I said we needed to mount a surveillance operation on Stellar, I should've specified the level of detail."

Lara sat back and folded her arms. "I'm new to this, remember? I only just found out that in another world I'm a superhero called Dark Trucker."

"Dark *Flutter*."

She nodded with fresh understanding. "Ahh, that explains her complete lack of haulage superpowers."

Back at the tree house I'd explained to her all about Dark Flutter and Stellar and Zack. And Zorbon the Decider and gerbil-holes and Gordon the World-Eater. Once she'd stopped walking in circles with a dazed look repeating "No way," she'd pulled herself together and asked if I had a plan.

Of course I did. First, we would track down Stellar, then stick to him like his own shadow. At some point he would be sure to lead us to Zack.

"After your – *his* – house was destroyed," Lara told me, "Luke and his family moved to a rented one on the edge of the park. That's where he'll be."

We stopped at Lara's house to pick up transport. Lara had a new Raleigh with 21 speed twist grip gears, and she lent me her old bike, which was too small for her, and a bit embarrassing for me. I'd kept up as best as I could. It wasn't just my bike that was wobbling, it felt like the entire multiverse had been knocked off balance by Stellar's vaulting ambition. (*Vaulting ambition* was a phrase I'd learned in Mr Bonnick's English class, which surprisingly had nothing to do with gymnastics, and more with the large-scale plans of Shakespearean villains.)

My only comfort was that Stellar's kidnap plan had a big problem. Even if he played the classic Zack-wasn't-really-killed-by-the-asteroid-but-had-amnesia card, his plan was a non-starter unless he could persuade Zack to go along with it. And my brother would never do that. Would he? I could already feel poky fingers of doubt. What with risk assessment and data protection requirements, hadn't he complained that he was fed up with life as Star Lad in our world? Here, he could give up being a superhero altogether and let Stellar do the job. And everyone Zack knew and loved already existed in this other Bromley – all just the same, more or less. Then there were the added bonuses of moving here. Hadn't Stellar suggested that Zack and Cara were boyfriend and girlfriend in this world?

Now that I understood Stellar's ultimate goal, his actions in my world began to make more sense. Protecting Star Lad's true identity, saving me from Wayne the laser-gerbil; every feat had the same aim – to impress Zack. Every deed said choose me. Even his accidental summoning of Gordon the World-Eater had ended up with him playing the hero. There was little doubt in my mind – Stellar had proved himself to be a better version of me. And that raised a fresh set of questions. What if I couldn't persuade Zack to come home? What if he chose to stay here? Would he even miss me?

When Lara and I arrived at Stellar's house I'd half expected it to be some kind of fortress with an electrified fence, guard towers and a black flag flying from his bedroom turret, but instead it was just an ordinary semi-detached house with pebbledash walls and a dormer. We'd secreted ourselves behind the bush and settled in to wait. It wasn't long before he returned home.

"Why didn't he tell me he was a superhero?" Lara sounded hurt. "I thought we were friends."

She obviously hadn't read many comics. "It's standard operating procedure. You don't tell anyone your secret identity."

"Your brother did. He told you."

"That was different. He hadn't a clue what he was doing. He needed my expertise."

"And then you told the other Lara and Serge."

There wasn't time to go into the whole Christopher Talbot kidnap saga, so I just said, "It was complicated."

"You mean there were insinuating circumstances," she said sagely. "That's when you do something different from what you're supposed to."

I was pretty sure that "circumstances" were usually "extentuating", but I found it comforting to know that this Lara was just like her counterpart in my world.

She gestured to the kitchen window. "Eagle One is on the move."

"Who's Eagle One?"

"It's my codename for Stellar," she said. "In situations like this don't you always have codenames?"

"Can't we just call him Stellar?"

"OK." She gave a reluctant sigh. "*Stellar* is getting up from the dinner table. He is putting his plate in the dishwasher..."

He disappeared from the kitchen and a minute later his bedroom light flicked on.

"He's probably doing his homework," said Lara.

"Or reading a comic." I figured that was the more likely option.

"Either way, he's in for the night."

I had to agree – Stellar wasn't leading us to Zack tonight. We called off the surveillance and made our way back to her house.

"If we're going to keep eyes on him at all times then we need more boots on the ground."

"You need boots for eyes?" said Lara. "This is all very strange."

"It's the only way to be sure he'll lead us to Zack. In my world I can call on the services of S.C.A.R.F., the

Superhero Covert Alliance Reaction Force."

"Is that some kind of top secret military outfit?" asked Lara.

"Uh, no, it's you, Zack, me and Serge."

"Serge?" She recoiled. "Serge LeFlaive? The most feared bully in school?"

"The what? No, there must be some mistake."

Lara shook her head slowly. "When Giles Pedlar cut in front of him in the dinner queue, Serge dismantled his mountain bike then turned the pieces into a sculpture and called it *le vélo triste*." Her voice fell to a hush. "The sad bicycle."

"That doesn't sound like—"

"And when Debz Holland refused to give him her maths homework to copy, he reduced her to a quivering wreck with a sonnet. Some of those rhymes were brutal." She shivered at the memory.

"OK, I agree, that's not very ni—"

"And last term he hacked into Susan Becker's phone," she went on, "so that every time she took a selfie, it changed her into a fat Mona Lisa."

"But he's my best friend," I said.

"He was, at one time. But no longer. And now the one person he hates more than anyone else is you."

Me? Why me, of all people? This Serge had taken a

very different path from the one I knew. I wondered what had turned him to the Dark Side.

"Promise me you'll stay out of his way," said Lara.

After that description it wasn't as if I was about to suggest he and I rent a tandem and go on a cycling holiday.

We arrived back at Lara's house. She said I must be tired and hungry after my trans-dimensional journey and I should come in and eat something. I was going to refuse on the grounds that her family might suspect I was a traveller from another universe, but after seeing Stellar tuck away all those sausages I was famished. I figured it was worth the risk.

"Is that you, Lara?" her mum called from the kitchen as we came through the front door.

"Hi, Mum," she replied. "Luke's here too." She hung up her coat and lowered her voice. "Cara might act a bit funny around you. Luke hasn't been here much since, y'know, what happened to Zack. It's possible that when she sees you she'll cry, hug you, or both."

I had a thought. "Maybe we could tell her what's going on. We need all the help we can get. And in my world Cara was highly resourceful in our fight against alien invaders."

Lara wrinkled her nose. "I don't think that's a good

idea – her teenage brain might explode. They're very unstable, from what I've observed. Personally, I am not relishing the onslaught of hormones."

Dinner passed uneventfully. There was no crying, hugging or indeed exploding, just shepherd's pie and apple crumble. To my surprise, Lara's parents were still happily together. This world might have been worse for my family, but it was clearly a happier place for the Lees. Or, at least, most of them. Cara sat through the meal in silence. She didn't call me "kid", which she did where I came from; in fact, she barely looked at me. I felt bad for her. It was obvious that she missed Zack, and my presence at dinner had only served to bring home his absence. I wondered if there was anything I could say to help.

I lowered my spoon. "Have you ever thought that in another universe things turned out differently?"

Cara looked up. "What?"

"Well, for instance, what if in a parallel world Zack wasn't killed?"

Cara stiffened. Lara's mum and dad exchanged anxious looks.

"And, what if, in that world, you're there too. And you don't even like him much. So you wouldn't be that sad even if he did get killed."

"Uh, Luke…" It was Lara. I think she shook her head, but it was such a tiny movement I couldn't be sure, so I ploughed on.

"And while you're not interested in him, Zack likes you. Even though for some reason he can't bring himself to tell you. What I'm trying to say is… It's all right. Somewhere out there, in a galaxy far, far away, it's all OK. Maybe that's not much, but y'know, it's something. I think."

There was a long pause, and then Cara laid her hand on mine.

With nothing to show for our efforts, Lara and I called a halt to the surveillance operation and I settled down in the tree house for the evening. I felt bad for the old place. In my world it was S.C.A.R.F. central command, echoing to the busy feet of superheroes and their back-up team countering the latest global threat (so long as it originated in Bromley). In this world the tree house looked like it had been abandoned since the asteroid strike. Stellar obviously didn't use it any more. Apart from some discarded chocolate wrappers it was dark and empty. Lara brought me a sleeping bag, a few supplies and a bunch of board games, in case I got bored. She didn't have any comics, the closest thing being an edition of Doctor Who Monopoly.

"Skaro, planet of the Daleks," I said, as her Tardis piece landed on my property. We'd been playing for a while and I was winning, for a change. "You owe me two hundred pounds."

She counted out the money. "I've been thinking. Even if you find Zack, how will you get home? It's not as if you can create a gerbil-hole and travel through it like Stellar."

"And neither could he, when he arrived in my world. Without me, he can't make the holes."

"So how did he travel to your world in the first place?"

"Stole Zorbon the Decider's ship," I said, rolling the dice. "He told me. Classic supervillain error, giving it away like that. Six!" I moved my sonic screwdriver token six places.

"Go To Jail," said Lara as I landed on the square in question. "But how does that help – if the ship is in your universe and you're here?"

I had it all figured out. "All I have to do is contact S.C.A.R.F. They'll locate the abandoned ship, then pilot it here to rescue us."

Lara still wasn't satisfied. "OK, but how do you plan on contacting them in another universe? It's not like you can call using Other Lara's phone."

"I can't, but Zack can. His telepathic power isn't

restricted by the gulf of space-time. Once he's back to full power he can reach out with his thoughts."

"Really? How do you know that?"

"Comics," I said. She shot me a doubtful look, which I ignored.

We wrapped up the game of Monopoly. It was time for Lara to head home. Tomorrow was Sunday and we agreed to recommence our hunt for Zack's hiding place at first light, or possibly after breakfast. Lara stopped in the doorway and stood there in uneasy silence.

"Everything OK?" I went to see what had unsettled her.

A sliver of the setting sun was missing. Of course, it hadn't actually gone anywhere, it was just obscured. "It's only an eclipse," I said.

"Don't look directly at it," she warned. "It's weird. Usually things like eclipses are all over the news before they occur. There's been no mention of this one."

As she said it I felt a shiver that wasn't caused by the cold evening air. I recalled that in olden times people feared eclipses, but not because of the damage they could do to your vision. They thought monsters were devouring the sun, or trying to steal it.

"It's probably nothing to worry about," she said.

But neither of us believed her.

As we stood there the air filled with a long, drawn-out hiss, as if some giant snake had slithered into the garden. From my vantage point in the door of the tree house I could see the source of the sound. Dozens of stray cats congregated on the street, hissing up at the broken sun.

24
OH NUTZ

Unzipping my sleeping bag I sat up and stretched. Instead of its typical warm, golden glow, the sunlight that slid into the tree house appeared washed out. Sickly. I went to the doorway and craned my neck to look east.

The sun glared low in the sky like an infected eye. The shadow from last night had spread so that a quarter of the sun was engulfed in darkness. By now a regular eclipse would have completed its crossing, which meant that this was something else. No doubt something very bad.

I went back inside, pulled on my clothes and broke open the supplies Lara had left me for breakfast.

Unfortunately, it was the last two boxes of cereal from a Variety pack and they were both Multi-Grain Rice Krispies. I was about to force them down when I was interrupted by the sound of humming from the garden. It was a cheerless tune, and also vaguely familiar.

With a creak the top of the rope ladder tensed. Someone was climbing up.

The dismal humming drew closer. I looked around for an alternative exit, but the tree house was strictly one way in and out. I decided that if I ever got home again I'd install an escape hatch in mine, but for now I was trapped.

A mane of perfectly styled hair crested the edge of the tree house landing, followed by a face I knew all too well. *Serge*.

Except that this wasn't my best friend – it was Evil Serge. We set eyes on one another at the same time and he instantly stopped humming.

Evil Serge regarded me with a mixture of curiosity and suspicion. He was carrying a takeaway cup on which was balanced a large slab of chocolate brownie. Placing both down carefully, he attempted to cross from the ladder to the tree house. As he stepped off, the ladder swayed to one side and he lurched awkwardly, leaving one foot on the top rung, one hand clawing the wooden deck. With a grunt he finally spanned the gap and flopped on the deck like a haddock. He may have been evil, but I was relieved to see that he and my Serge displayed the same level of physical prowess. Face down like that I saw he was wearing a backpack themed with a colourful image of supervillain Two-Face. Which felt like a bad sign.

He jumped to his feet, collected his hot beverage and brownie, and brushed down what looked like a silk waistcoat.

Neither of us spoke. From what Lara had told me of his rep (when you have a reputation as fearsome as Evil Serge's it's called a *rep*), I was in serious trouble.

He broke the silence. "This morning I stopped by Bean Me Up, Scottie for my usual Sunday order." He held up the cup and brownie. "Constellation Class Hot Chocolate with a Photon Chocpedo." He plucked the brownie off the lid and took a sip of the drink. "While there I spotted someone else in the queue. Can you guess who that might have been?"

I shook my head.

"Luke. Parker." He raised one eyebrow. "Can you explain this?"

"That might take a while."

Serge nibbled the end of the brownie. "Then allow me to speculate on the various possibilities. One – it was you. You collected your breakfast combo, rushed back here and, for whatever reason would possess you, changed into these clothes." He sneered at my choice of sweatshirt. "Two – I have stumbled into some multiverse monkey business and you are an identical Luke Parker from a different world. Which means either you are my most detested foe, or his entirely innocent double from another dimension."

"*That* one! I'm the innocent one!" I insisted. He took a step towards me and I shrank back, blurting out the reason for my presence. "Stellar kidnapped my brother from my world and I came to yours to rescue him."

If Evil Serge was anything at all like mine, then he was the one person in this universe who might accept my hurried and extraordinary explanation without a shred of evidence. I could see him weighing it up.

His free hand moved quickly, delving into a pocket. I flinched in expectation at what he might pull out. To my relief I saw it was his inhaler.

"My name is Serge LeFlaive. I could have been *un super-héros*, but I was betrayed." He took a suck of Ventolin. "By Luke Parker."

Serge and I sat in the tree house among Lara's collection of board games. He removed his Two-Face backpack and set it down next to him.

"I come here every Sunday. Sometimes I listen to my music, or read, but mostly I come to remember." He sighed. "Once, Luke and I were friends. Best friends, or so I believed. We shared a common love of comics."

So far, so identical.

"I was with him for the final battle between Cap and Red Skull in *Captain America* number 300. I was with him for the unveiling of Superior Spider-Man's new costume. And I was with him on the fateful evening when Zorbon the Decider visited for the first time."

That was not how it had played out in my world. "Then you know that he's Stellar."

He nodded. "I believe that I am the only one."

I informed him that Lara was in on the secret now, but something puzzled me about his version of the story. "So if you were in the tree house when Zorbon was giving out powers, then how come you're not a superhero too?"

His nostrils flared, a vein stood out on his temple and he muttered a stream of angry French words. "Treachery," he spat. "Faced with the glowing majesty of Zorbon the Decider, I reacted as any normal person would. I felt an asthma attack coming on. But when I searched for my inhaler, it was nowhere to be found. Then Luke announced that he remembered seeing it back in the house, on the kitchen table. So, immediately I climbed down and went to look. The inhaler was not in the kitchen. Thankfully, the attack came to nothing and soon I was able to return to the tree house. But when I got there, Zorbon was gone – and Luke had superpowers." He stopped to draw breath. "And there was my inhaler. It had been in the tree house all along. Luke claimed to have found it after I left, hidden beneath an issue of *Fantastic Four*." Serge squeezed the chocolate brownie in his fist. "*Menteur!* Liar! He wanted the powers all for himself."

I wondered how I would've reacted in the same circumstances. I hoped I'd have been happy for Serge to become a superhero too, but what if it had been an either/or situation? I didn't like to think what I would have done to ensure that I was the Chosen One.

"Is it possible Luke was telling the truth?" I suggested, fearful of provoking another angry outburst. "Maybe you really did misplace it."

Serge shook his head. "I too could have been a superhero, except that *my friend* hid my inhaler." He paused. "And now, with your assistance, I will have my revenge."

"Uh, it's not really a vengeance thing I'm going for," I said. "It has more of a rescue flavour."

I studied my alternate-world best friend as he downed his hot chocolate and squished brownie. I felt sure that this Serge would prove to be a formidable ally in any confrontation with Stellar. He may not possess actual superpowers but his mere presence instilled fear, which was pretty close. And vengeance has always been a great motivator for super-characters. Batman, Robin, Doctor Doom, Punisher, the list is endless. Although, when I thought about it, those feelings didn't exactly make for the most healthy, well-adjusted people.

"Uh, Luke, are you OK?" Lara's quizzical voice came from the doorway. She peered in at us. Her mouth hung open and then she pressed her lips together in puzzlement. Fair to say she had not expected to find me and the most feared bully in school shooting the breeze. I could tell that a jumble of questions was whizzing through her mind.

"It's OK, he's on our side," I said, quickly explaining Serge's presence. I turned to him. "You are, right?"

He gave a less than enthusiastic shrug and unzipped his backpack.

"Great," said Lara nervously. "The more help the better, right?"

There was a skitter of claws as something moved among the board games, upsetting the neat stack. They

223

toppled to the floor.

Lara flinched and shut her eyes. "Please tell me it isn't a rat."

It wasn't. The offending creature hopped into full view.

"*Un écureuil?*" said Serge.

I assumed that was French for squirrel, because that's what it was: a bushy tailed grey squirrel. I would've said it was staring right at me, but since its eyes are on the side of its head it was more of a sideways look. "Maybe it lives here," I said.

"You mean it's a homing squirrel?" Lara nodded thoughtfully. "Do you get those?"

"*Non*, I come to the tree house every week," said Serge, "and have never before seen this creature."

It began to circle the fallen board games. If I didn't know better I'd have said it was searching for something. With a whirl of paws it dislodged one of the boxes and thumped its tail on the fallen cover.

"Scrabble?" I said. The squirrel lifted its head and looked at me as if it understood.

"What are you doing?" asked Lara dubiously. "You know it can't understand you, right?"

"In my universe Dark Flutter is always surrounded by small woodland creatures. I wonder…" I removed the board from the box and deposited the letter tiles next to it. No sooner had I done so than the squirrel nosed a letter on to the board, quickly following it with several more. A jumble of letters grew across the board. I sounded them out. "I.S.T.H. I.S.T.H. I.N. G.O.N. That's complete nonsense." I was disappointed, although I'm not sure what I'd expected.

Serge reached past me. Without changing the order of the letters, he adjusted how they were grouped. I sounded them out once more.

"I.S. T.H.I.S. T.H.I.N.G. O.N." No way. *"Is this thing on?"*

Lara gasped. "I don't believe it."

The squirrel's nose twitched and then it bounded back to the pile of letters, pushing another batch on to the board.

S.C.A.R.F.I.S.H.E.R.E.

"Scarfish 'ere?" Lara pored over the letters.

This time I knew what it was trying to spell. "S.C.A.R.F. is here," I mouthed, turning excitedly to the others. "It's the Superhero Covert Alliance Reaction Force. On a triple-word score!" Somehow my Lara was using her Dark Flutter powers to communicate from her universe to this one, through the squirrel. My friends had found me.

"L.U.K.E.   W.E.   H.A.V.E.   V.I.T.A.L. I.N.F.O.R.M.A.T.I.O.N."

There was a short delay as the squirrel gathered more letters.

"O.I. N.O. T.A.I.L. G.I.M.M.E. N.U.T.Z." That didn't seem terribly vital, unless you were a squirrel. There was a pause and then more letters.

"S.O.R.R.Y. A.B.O.U.T. T.H.A.T."

Dark Flutter must have regained control. Another sentence took shape.

"I.T. I.S. T.H.E. E.N.D. O.F. T.H.E. W.O.R.D."

Well, that wasn't too bad. Of all the disasters that could have befallen us, that seemed fairly low on the list. Out of the corner of my eye I spotted the squirrel pushing one more letter towards the board. It deposited the final tile and sat back. I reviewed the altered sentence.

I.T. I.S. T.H.E. E.N.D. O.F. T.H.E. W.O.R.L.D.

25
THE COSMIC JENGA
CALAMITY THEORY

There were only ninety-eight letter tiles in the Scrabble box (plus two blanks), which meant we had to endure a painstaking wait for the squirrel to spell out S.C.A.R.F.'s shocking discovery. It took long enough that formerly Evil Serge moved on to his next meal of the day. He dug out a Magneto-themed lunch box from his backpack and popped the lid. It was like unsealing the ancient tomb of someone who'd been buried with a lot of fish.

Lara pinched her nose. "What is that smell?"

Serge lifted out a pile of bread doorsteps and assessed their filling. "Egg and anchovy," he said. "Ugh. What is this?" He drew out a Babybel cheese snack.

"Where is my Brie?"

I returned my attention to the Scrabble board. It seemed that the Serge in my universe had sifted through all the parallel-world storylines in comics he could find and, drawing on his extensive reading, had come up with a theory about the gerbil-holes.

"I don't get it," said Lara, scanning the board when the squirrel had finally finished. "Obviously I haven't read enough comics."

I rooted through the rest of the games. "I think this will help to explain," I said, removing a box from the stack.

"Jenga?" she said.

"It's the best way to represent in a simple and clear fashion what's going on," I said. "It was either this, or Connect 4."

I made space on the floor and assembled a tower of wooden blocks. "Now, imagine this is the multiverse," I said. "Here's what happens when Stellar pulls an object from another universe." Carefully, I slid out one wooden block from the middle of the tower. It remained upright. I eased out another. This time the tower wobbled but held in place. "Each time Stellar creates a gerbil-hole, the risk increases. It might be the next hole, or the one after that, but at some point…" I whipped out a block from the base of the tower. It swayed once and collapsed in a clicking cascade.

"He is turning the multiverse into Emmental," said Serge. "It is a holey cheese."

"Like Jarlsberg?" asked Lara.

"It is firm like Jarlsberg but exhibits a nutty flavour."

Serge had ignored my excellent Jenga comparison in order to go dairy instead, but this version of my friend still scared me, so I didn't object. And anyway, he was essentially correct.

With the squirrel's revelation our mission hadn't changed, but now there was an additional objective. "We have to rescue my brother," I said. "And we have to do so while preventing Stellar from creating any more holes in the universe."

What was already a tall order had just doubled in height. Lara gagged at the whiff rising from Serge's sandwiches. "I need some fresh air."

We followed her out on to the tree-house deck. From our vantage we had a view over the surrounding streets. The partially eclipsed sun shed an uneasy half-light across the rooftops.

"Somewhere out there Stellar is holding Zack." Lara swept an arm to the horizon. "The question is where?"

The problem was he could be anywhere. Perhaps not

even in Bromley. Stellar could easily have flown him halfway across the world. If this were a board game, we were on square one.

As difficult as the challenge was that faced us, I wasn't about to give up. "It would have to be somewhere far from starlight so that Zack can't recharge his powers." I thought back to my arrival in this world. "And somewhere that would muffle his telepathy."

"A nuclear bunker?" said Serge.

"In Bromley?" Lara dismissed the suggestion.

Serge offered another possibility. "Per'aps an undersea lair?"

"There's the Pavilion Leisure Centre," said Lara. "It has a pool."

It wasn't the worst idea. After all, the Alien Overlord's mothership had been disguised as a secondary school, and the last supervillain I'd encountered based himself in a comic shop designed to look like a volcano.

"If I was Stellar," mused Lara, "where would I hide Zack?"

"That is not the question." Serge pressed a finger to my chest. "If *you* were Stellar…"

"Yes, of course!" Lara leapt on his suggestion. "You two are the same. You think alike. The answer is in your head."

Ever since Stellar had arrived in my world I'd protested to anyone who'd listen that he and I were not the same person, but maybe she was on to something.

Lara gripped my shoulders and fixed me in the eye. "To trap the squirrel you must think like one."

To find my brother I had to think myself into Stellar's mind. So, if I was a supervillain, where would *I* keep a superhero under wraps?

I closed my eyes and in my head began to repeat the same phrase over and over.

"I am Stellar."

My body remained at the tree house but my mind began to drift. Soon I was above the wasteland of the garden looking down on rats picking over scraps. Out over Moore Street I flew, the mewing of stray cats rising up from the weed-torn pavement. Strange winds blew me across the park. And then I was floating along the High Street.

I heard Serge and Lara's distant voices.

"Think evil."

"Are your minds melding yet?"

I shut them out and redoubled my efforts.

I am Stellar. I am Stellar.

I drifted higher, edging towards the black of the eclipse, which extended like an endless tunnel through the blue sky.

A tunnel!

I blinked. I was back. Lara and Serge's expectant faces greeted me. I grinned. I knew where Stellar was holding Zack.

"He's in the Batcave."

★★★

26
THE DARK NIGHT

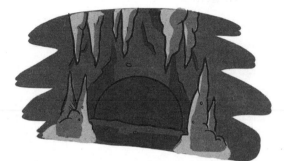

I inspected the cave entrance for signs of fresh footprints. The dirt surface was as smooth as I'd left it. No one had been in, or out. Before I went deeper in I glanced up at the eclipse. It was all over the news. The world had woken to the ping of alerts across every device. After what happened with Nemesis, people were understandably twitchy. To the world's collective relief another rogue asteroid had been ruled out. The experts who'd been wheeled out to comment on the phenomenon all agreed that this was not a typical solar eclipse, when the moon passes between the sun and Earth. However, none of the talking heads could come up with a reasonable explanation for what was going on. I didn't know either, but I hoped it was a sign that something wicked was on its way to Earth. I was longing for an army of evil space slugs. Zack and I needed to bond. What better way than by teaming up to battle a slimy global threat?

I collected the lamp from the alcove and set off down the narrow, sloping tunnel into the gloom. As I made my way around stalactites and stalagmites, the swinging lamp-light throwing shadows against the walls, I felt a presence in the darkness. Not a ghost or a cave-monster, but something far more unsettling. It had loomed over me since my first meeting with Other Luke, a question as unavoidable as Karnak the Inhuman's giant head.

Was I the Evil Twin?

In comics there are superheroes who start off with good intentions, but somewhere down the road everything gets twisted. They lose their way. I never intended to be the bad guy. Everything I'd done – stealing Zorbon's ship, kidnapping Zack from another universe – I'd done for good reasons. I just wanted to make Mum and Dad and all the people who loved my brother happy again. I wanted to be happy again. I was sure I'd come across a phrase that summed it up: the ends justify being mean. So had I lost my way? I was too far down this road to go back now, so I pushed the question back into the shadows. However, if my destiny was to don the black cape of villainy, I resolved to avoid making some obvious mistakes.

I reached the archway that led to the chamber where I'd locked Zack up. I was pleased to find the force field securely in place, emitting a powerful hum. It didn't actually need to hum, since electrical humming is caused by stray magnetic fields making transformers vibrate, and there was no transformer. But I liked the effect.

I parted the field and went inside. I'd brought him something to eat and a change of clothes. He'd arrived in my world wearing his Star Lad costume but I could hardly reintroduce him to Mum and Dad wearing that. I was also carrying a secret weapon. Not a weapon like a power ring or a lasso of truth; this was a family photo album. I hoped that seeing pictures of us together would bring him round to the idea that we really were his family.

Zack lay on the floor of the cave, doing sit-ups by the light of the glow-sticks I'd left him.

I set down the takeaway from the café next to him. "I got you a meal combo. A medium Chai-ly Illogical, Wrap of Khan and one To Boldly Doughnut."

He completed another sit-up and counted, "One hundred and sixty-four."

He was pretending to ignore me. Which was typical of Zack.

"And I thought we could look through this together," I said, opening the album.

"One hundred and sixty-five."

"So many memories." I turned the pages, thick with snapshots of our family.

"One hundred and sixty-six."

"Oh, you must remember this one – when we went to that safari park and I tried to smuggle out a monkey?"

He stopped exercising and sat up, breathing lightly. "Nope." He dabbed his forehead with a sleeve. "I'm sorry, but while I accept that in some ways I am him, I'm also *not* him."

"Don't say that!"

"I know what you're trying to do," he said, gesturing to the album. "And it won't work."

"I can make you remember. There are other ways of changing people's minds," I said darkly, closing the album with a thud. "Mind control, for instance."

Zack got slowly to his feet. I could see that I'd rattled him. "You have mind-control powers?"

OK, well, now this was a bit awkward. "Uh, no. But I reckon I could give it a good try. It's kind of like evil telepathy, right?"

Zack sighed. "You are *so* like him."

"Yes! Yes I am," I said, seizing upon his admission. "I *am* Luke. And you *are* Zack."

He stood in silence and then he laid a hand on my shoulder. For a second I thought he was about to attempt a judo throw, but then a sad smile appeared on his face.

"What happened wasn't your fault," he said. "You can't save everyone."

"You did."

"I had help. Without Luke and his friends, that day would've ended differently. You took on Nemesis all by yourself."

"I had to. First rule of being a superhero – keep your identity a secret."

"Sorry." He gave me a sheepish look. "I broke that one. Maybe you should break it too. This thing we do, it's a gift, but it's also a heavy responsibility. You should think about sharing it."

"And if I do, will you stay? Just tell me – what will it take to convince you?"

For a moment I thought he was about to give me an answer, but instead he shook his head. "I could lie to you. Say that I've come round. But it wouldn't be fair – to either of us."

I stamped my foot, sending up a cloud of dirt. "Your

choice. But we are deep underground. No starlight can reach you here. And until you accept that you are my brother, I can't let you leave."

Zack put his hands on his hips and cast his eye around the cavern. "Are we in Chislehurst Caves?"

First rule of supervillainy – never tell them your plan. "Maybe."

He ran a hand along one wall as he proceeded to walk round the perimeter. "I know this place. This is where Dad took us when Luke wanted a Batcave." I could see it all come back to him. "Yeah, and when he turned off the lamp, Luke freaked out."

Barely had he spoken the words when my head began to throb. Something had triggered my Stellar Scanner. A blurry image swam into my mind. Three figures dismounting from bikes at the cave entrance. I homed in on them and gasped. Other Luke was here, in my world. But how? There wasn't time to speculate. He was not alone. I adjusted the image until they came into focus. It was Lara Lee. Of course, they were best friends in his universe. At least in this one she didn't have superpowers. And the third? Serge! Well, how about that. Somehow Other Luke had patched it up with him.

"Luke?" muttered Zack.

I spun round. I could see it in his face – Zack had

detected his other brother. But how? Unless he was using his Star-Sense, which was – "Impossible. You're out of starlight and there's no way you could have recharged your powers."

Zack gave an apologetic shrug. "Surprise?"

27
STAR LAD vs STELLAR

The entrance to the cave lay before us. A few hundred metres inside, at the end of its twisting passageways, my brother was being held captive by Stellar – I was sure of it. For the first time since arriving in this world I had an advantage over my Evil Twin: he didn't know we were coming.

"You ready?" I asked the others.

Lara nodded and a smile played about her lips. "We have the elephant of surprise."

"*Um*, yeah, it's the *element* of surprise."

She snorted. "That's ridiculous. What does that even mean? An elephant makes much more sense. What would you do if you felt a tap on your shoulder, then turned round to find a wrinkly trunk belonging to a blinking great elephant standing behind you?"

"Leap three metres straight up in the air?" said Serge.

"Exactly."

She had a point.

I was about to lead us into the cave when there was the whistle of parting air.

"Watch out!" Lara dropped to the ground as, with a crunch of exploding rock, two figures shot out of the narrow cave entrance. Splinters of stone rained down on us. I looked up from my prone position.

Twisting around each other in a subsonic streak, Stellar and Star Lad cleared the treetops and arrowed into the darkening sky.

"Zack's escaped!" cried Lara delightedly.

"Typical," I muttered. It was *so typical* of my brother. We'd just visited the cave shop and I'd bought supplies. I had a whole Mission Impossible rescue plan figured out, involving glow-sticks, multiple pulleys and a particularly imaginative use of a karabiner. And what does Zack do? Ruin it.

Lara was already on her bike, racing back towards the car park, tracking the figures in the sky. I hopped on to mine and set after her, gawping at the scene unfolding

241

above. Star Lad and Stellar were locked in single combat. I'd witnessed a lot of fantastic things lately, from giant robots in shopping centres to alien motherships to world-eating monsters, but here was something which until that moment I'd only seen in comics or films: a battle between superpowered foes wearing capes.

"This is the best thing *ever*," said Serge, voicing my unspoken thought. "*Incroyable!* Although, I struggle with the idea that in any universe Zack Parker is *le superheros*."

"I know. Annoying, isn't it?"

We pedalled furiously to keep pace with the action. There was the sound of wrenching metal as a lamppost tore itself from the pavement and flew narrowly over our heads. All along the road a line of lampposts ripped themselves from their foundations and speared into the air.

Controlling them with telekinesis, Stellar launched the posts at Star Lad. I could see my brother track the incoming projectiles and in an instant activate his force field. They bounced off his protective shield and tumbled back to earth. Star Lad had enough presence of mind to guide them safely down, making sure to avoid innocent bystanders, although a parked Ford Focus got one in the sunroof.

It was Star Lad's turn to launch a telekinetic attack of his own. Swooping low, he skimmed over a row of bungalows. As he sped past them there was a tearing noise and the houses' perfectly manicured lawns detached themselves from their roots and followed in his wake.

"Why is he doing that?" asked Lara.

I realised the genius of his manoeuvre. "I have hay fever," I said. "Which means –"

"– so does Stellar," she finished.

Gaining altitude, Star Lad opened fire on his opponent with a rapid burst of bungalow lawn. Stellar disappeared beneath the onslaught, swamped by a green carpet. We awaited the inevitable sneeze-pocalypse.

"And that's what you call a *turf war*," I quipped. But unfortunately Lara didn't hear me over the rumble of thunder that immediately filled the sky. The ground shook beneath our wheels.

Stellar had opened a gerbil-hole.

"Stellar, listen to me," I shouted the words in my head. "If you don't stop what you're doing you risk triggering the end of all existence. Your gerbil-holes are altering the structure of the multiverse."

There was a pause, and then to my surprise, I heard him.

"Is it like Emmental?"

For flip's sake, what was it with the cheese similes?

He gave a mocking laugh. "Nice try, Other Luke, but you don't honestly expect me to fall for that one, do you? It's the oldest trick in the comic book – *your powers threaten the very fabric of space-time.* I mean, come on, really, is that the best you've got?" His voice whispered in my head. "Let me show you what I've got." And with that, he severed our telepathic link.

"Incoming!" Lara yelled.

A fleet of lawn tractors blasted out of the latest gerbil-hole, cutting decks lowered, blades spinning. But these were no ordinary tractors. Each came equipped with what I estimated to be a 50-litre grass-cutting collector, and a thrust vectoring nozzle and lift fan like the one on the F-35 Joint Strike Fighter. The flying tractors tore through the lawns, which fell in clods all around us, setting off car alarms, sending passers-by seeking shelter in doorways. Stellar shrugged off the last few blades of grass, sent the tractors back through the hole and set off again in pursuit of my brother.

There was still enough illumination from the eclipsed sun to pick out the two of them. Light rolled off Stellar's cape as he zoomed past us at low level, gesturing to a row of terraced houses. The air filled with a hum like a swarm of angry bees. All the satellite dishes on the houses vibrated, and with a series of pings broke free from their mountings, racing skyward like an alien saucer fleet on an intercept course with Star Lad.

He picked them off one by one, swiftly targeting them with his Star-Sense radar, then knocking them out of the sky with a volley of pinpoint telekinetic blasts.

From our position on the ground Star Lad and Stellar were, at that exact moment, perfectly framed by what remained of the sun. By then it was half in light, half in darkness. Like the two halves, the opponents were evenly matched.

"They're heading to the shops," said Lara, speeding after the flying gladiators.

The battle went street to street, cul-de-sac to avenue. At one moment Star Lad gained the upper hand, then the advantage switched to Stellar. There was a brief but violent exchange of seafood over the fishmonger. It was a clever move on Stellar's part, since Zack hated prawns.

Stellar used his gerbil-hole power again. This time hundreds of sheets of paper streamed out of the dimensional portal and surrounded my brother. Stray sheets floated to the ground. I braked and leaned down to collect a bundle. This was bad. Really bad. "Exam papers."

Serge made a face. "Is that all?"

"You don't understand – they appear to be exam papers for the *next three years*." I looked up at my brother, knowing what was about to happen.

"He's closed his eyes," said Lara. "Why's he doing that?"

I knew why. My scrupulously honest brother didn't want to risk glimpsing the questions and gaining an unfair advantage in a future exam. Stellar was a genius. But as my Evil Twin moved in to take advantage, Star Lad began to spin at an incredible rate. In seconds he had created a vortex that sucked in the exam papers, whirled them around furiously and spat them out. Thousands of paper ribbons drifted on the breeze. He had shredded the exam questions, not only removing the immediate threat to him, but ensuring no one could benefit from Stellar's cheating.

The battle raged and each time Stellar opened a hole it caused a new and stronger tremor. The universe continued to exist. For now.

I caught up to Lara and Serge and the three of us pedalled side by side.

"It's too dangerous to let him carry on making those holes," I said.

Lara shook her head. "But how do we stop him?"

Before I could answer, something scurried out in front of my wheel and I slammed on the brakes. It was a rat. It darted across the road, pursued by a straggly-looking cat, a stray like those I'd seen roaming Moore Street.

I had an idea. "Serge, I have a vital question, the answer to which could very well make the difference between our mission succeeding and the end of the world – in every universe."

"*Oui?*"

"Did you eat all your sandwiches?"

Five minutes later Serge was on his way back to the tree house to carry out my plan. I couldn't have put my trust in anyone better. He had the grit, the determination and the anchovies. Meanwhile, as people realised that something extraordinary was happening above them, the streets filled with onlookers. At first they were unsure about the superpowered clash, but wariness quickly turned to excitement at the thrilling aerial action. With a screech of tyres, a pair of competing mobile TV news crews swung into the street from opposite ends, narrowly avoiding a collision with each other. The emergency services showed up too. There were fire engines, ambulances, even a police helicopter. A policeman with a loudhailer ordered Star Lad and Stellar to cease fighting, but I don't think anyone expected that they would actually listen, not even the policeman.

Hovering high above us, capes rippling out behind them, Star Lad and Stellar stared each other down like a couple of Wild West gunslingers.

I closed my eyes. "Zack, can you hear me?"

"My Star-Sense wasn't wrong – it *is* you. Bit busy right now, Luke."

I needed to tell Zack something but there was a chance Stellar was listening in. I had to take the risk. "Get to the tree house."

"You have a plan? Why am I asking – of course you have a plan. OK. See you there."

The battle resumed at the same breathless pace, but after a few more superpowered exchanges I could tell that the crowd's initial excitement was beginning to wane. The police and fire brigade were called to another emergency. People drifted away. Even the TV news crews drove off, having recorded enough superhero action for a feature film and eight sequels. I could completely understand their loss of enthusiasm. What is it with superhero fights that they always go on far too long?

By the time the trail of destruction led to Moore Street, we were the only interested civilians left following the battling supers. Zack was true to his word. He herded

Stellar along our street. They clashed above the garden at number 128 and then the two of them dropped from sight.

We ditched the bikes and squeezed through the gap in the fence that ringed Stellar's former home. For the first time since the fight began, the skies above Bromley were silent and empty. Surrounded by an eerie stillness we made our way across the blasted garden to the foot of the tree house. I clambered up the rope ladder and opened the door.

Stellar and Star Lad faced each other across a floor squirming with cats.

28
YOU MUST BE KITTEN ME

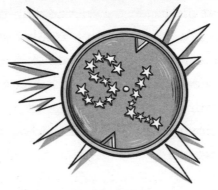

Cats packed the tree house, mewing, hissing and slinking. There wasn't a centimetre of floor space that didn't contain a paw or a hackle. Serge had accomplished the mission, even at the cost of triggering his allergies. He took several puffs of his inhaler and shook a ginger tom off one leg.

"Well, look at this, the gang's all here," Stellar sneered.

Lara folded her arms and met his gaze with a steely one of her own.

Stellar fixed me across the room. "Just in time for me to send you back where you came from," he crowed. "Bye-bye." Casually, he waved a hand to open a gerbil-hole.

Nothing happened.

He did it again, but with no more success. He tried the other hand, then both together, until he was whirling his arms like a windmill. I could see the confusion and panic in his face. He had lost his power, and didn't know why.

"It's the cats," I explained. "Everyone knows that when you tell a cat to do something, it completely ignores you. Even a superhero with animal powers can't get through. There's something about feline brainwaves that makes commands simply bounce off them. My plan counted on that. I was betting that if we stuck enough of them in one room it would turn it into a sort of Faraday cage." A Faraday cage was a container that blocked electric fields rather than superpowers but it was close enough.

Zack grinned. "Or, I suppose we ought to call it a *Fur*-aday cage."

"That was awful." I shuddered at the pun. "Or should I say *clawful*?"

We all winced. Even Stellar.

"Interesting," mused Lara. "It seems one side effect of being around so many cats is that you can't help making terrible cat puns."

A wiry Persian slunk past, eyeing me with what I could only describe as an amused expression. Their power was truly frightening.

"Ha! Well, I'm not staying around to find out," said Stellar. He bent his knees and sprang into the air.

Except that he didn't.

He rose a few centimetres and thudded back down. He tried again, but the cats pressed their furry bodies against him and he remained firmly stuck to the floor. An expression of dismay spread across his face as he realised he was powerless, in every sense. He let out a cry born of anger and frustration, his shoulders slumped and the fight seemed to go out of him.

I nodded to Serge. "Will you do the honours?"

As well as luring stray cats into the tree house with his last anchovy sandwich, Serge had carried out the other, less experimental, part of my plan and collected a chair from the remains of the house and a length of garden twine. He proceeded to tie Stellar to the chair.

"What about Catwoman?" said Stellar huffily. "She can control cats."

"That's because she's made up," sighed Lara. "There's a difference."

It was the first time she'd confronted her old friend since discovering his secret identity. I could tell she was upset. "Luke, how could you do this?"

"Luke who? I'm Stellar. Never heard of any Luke…"

"Oh, for goodness' sake." She ripped the mask from his face. There was no concealing the truth now. "You complete idiot. You should've told me."

He lowered his head. "There's nothing you can do. It's too late." He looked up at Serge. "First, I betrayed my best friend, and then I couldn't save the one person in the world who mattered to me. You know what that is, don't you?"

"It is the origin story of a supervillain," said Serge.

"Exactly. There's no point in fighting it."

"Maybe so, but we can try," insisted Lara. "And we're going to make a start, right now." She dragged Serge in front of the seated Stellar. "I want you two to make up."

The former friends regarded one another in suspicious silence.

Serge spoke first. "That night. My inhaler. You betrayed me like Superboy Prime betrayed the Justice League."

Stellar made a face. "It wasn't *that* bad."

"It was to me."

They held each other's gaze for a long time. "I'm sorry," said Stellar. And it sounded like he meant it.

I caught Zack staring at me. In all the fuss the significance of my presence was only now occurring to him. As the others talked among themselves and tried to patch things up, he pulled me into a corner of the tree house. I felt sure he was about to express his gratitude to me for braving a perilous cosmic journey to rescue him. I just hoped he wouldn't get too mushy.

"What are you even doing here?" A horrified expression came over his face. "Do Mum and Dad know you're in another dimension?"

Well, at least he didn't hug me. "Never mind Mum and Dad," I said. "What I want to know is how did you escape? Last time I saw you, you were doing a pretty good impersonation of a glove puppet minus the hand up its bum. And since then you've been stored in darkness like the last fish finger in the freezer."

Zack opened his hand. In his palm lay a credit-card-sized object emblazoned with his sigil. I'd seen it once before, in my world, when he'd been preparing to leave for Other Bromley. "Star Squad's research division has been working on this for me. Still a prototype, but it does the job."

I didn't understand. "You have your own line of credit cards?"

Zack gave a huff. He thumbed the sigil, which turned out to be a button. The credit card lit up with an intense light, the glare so bright that the rest of us had to shield our eyes.

"Synthetic star-light," he explained. "Nowhere near as powerful as the real thing, but useful in a pinch." He switched it off.

"It's a charger?"

"Yes, although not a quick one. My powers are still far from at their peak. I'd have preferred another day to replenish before I took on Stellar, but I hadn't counted on you showing up. And there was a lot to consider before I mounted any sort of escape attempt. For a start, how deep was I underground? Were the cave ceiling heights consistent and predictable, or was there a likelihood of bumping my head in a rapid breakout scenario? Could I get out without causing unnecessary injury to innocent civilians or damage to the historic surroundings? How could I overpower and then safely secure Stellar? That sort of thing."

It all sounded kind of familiar. "You did a risk assessment," I said.

Zack nodded. "Absolutely. It's only in a situation like that you understand just how valuable they can be."

More important than his stupid form-filling, there was something I had to know. "So you weren't tempted to stay in this world?"

Zack hesitated before he replied. But it was only to move back towards the others. He wanted to ensure that

Stellar could hear his next words.

"I don't belong here," he said. "I'm sorry."

I should have felt relief, but when I saw Stellar's face contort in pain, my stomach tightened like one of the knots holding him in place. There was something I had avoided confronting since the moment I learned of Stellar's plan to replace his brother with mine; an inescapable question as uncomfortable as Hawkman's chest straps.

Was what Stellar had done so evil?

On the one hand, yes. *Obviously.* He'd lied, abused his solemn superhero oath, summoned a world-eating terror during a hissy fit, kidnapped and imprisoned Zack. On the other hand, in comics and films when superheroes faced impossible odds, they moved Heaven and Earth to save their world. Stellar had moved *infinite* worlds to put things right for him and his family. And this was the big question – is it OK to do bad things if you're doing them to help the people you love? It had been much simpler to think of Stellar as my Evil Twin. It made the world an uncomplicated black and white. But suddenly that world, like my own, felt a long way away.

"So what's the plan for getting us home?" asked Zack. "I assume you have one."

I nodded. "But not here." Even though Stellar's

powers were neutralised, I didn't want to risk discussing it in front of him. "I just need a couple of things." Brushing off some cats, I collected the Scrabble board, Serge scooped up the squirrel, and we headed out of the tree house.

Darkness crept across the garden as I led the others to what used to be the garden shed, but which was now a cracked concrete foundation and a handful of splintered two-by-fours. I laid out the Scrabble board.

"Serge, the interdimensional squirrel, please."

He handed it to me.

"What are you doing?" questioned Zack.

"Establishing whether this creature can receive as well as send. Now, if you'll excuse me." I peered into its fluffy face. "Dark Flutter, if you can hear this, give me a sign." There was a pause, then its tail stood straight up and waggled about in a weird, non-squirrel-y fashion. "Excellent." I proceeded to inform the squirrel that Stellar had made a classic supervillain mistake when he told me about using Zorbon's ship to travel to our world. Then I'd put *två* and *två* together (*två* was Swedish for two) and come up with the likely location of the ship. "Look for it in IKEA." With my final instruction dispatched, I set the squirrel down next to the Scrabble board. Immediately it spelled out a reply.

W.E. W.I.L.L. F.I.N.D. I.T. A.N.D. C.O.M.E.
F.O.R. Y.O.U. B.E. R.E.A.D.Y.

A.L.S.O.

H.A.V.E. Y.O.U. G.O.T. M.Y. P.H.O.N.E.

Reading those words – well, the first lot – I was filled with hope. My friends were coming. And, of course, my friends were here too. Two Laras, two Serges and a Zack – there was no way we could fail. "It's only a matter of time until S.C.A.R.F. find the ship. In the meantime, Stellar is safely secured in the tree house, unable to create more gerbil-holes. The world, the universe, and indeed the entire multiverse is safe. All we have to do is wait to be picked up."

Zack gave a contented sigh. "Frankly, it's just a relief for once not to be racing against a giant flaming alien countdown in the sky. Good work, Luke."

I barely heard my brother's praise, because just then I noticed another new message on the Scrabble board.

A.R.E. Y.O.U. S.E.E.I.N.G. A.N. E.C.L.I.P.S.E.
T.O.O.

The squirrel crouched at the end of the sentence like a furry grey question mark. The eclipse was happening in my universe too. What did that mean? How could we both be seeing the same phenomenon? And then it hit me.

"Lara, do you have a notebook?"

"Of course." Her cub reporter's instincts never left her. She handed it to me and I tore out two pieces of paper.

"Zack, can I borrow your sigil?"

I'd made Star Lad's sigil out of one of Mum's old brooches. I used the pin to pierce a hole in the paper. "I know what's causing the eclipse," I said. "It's not a giant piece of Jenga or a galactic wedge of cheese."

Turning my back on the eclipse I held one piece of paper above my shoulder and used the second as a screen. An image of the sun appeared, projected through the pinhole. As I suspected. "It's a shadow."

"A shadow of what?" asked Zack.

"The universe next door." I tapped a finger against the paper image of the eclipse. "*Our* universe is about to crash into this one."

29
GOODBYE, MY SON

That morning I'd awoken to a sliver of black sun; now most of its surface had fallen into shadow. Like the *Titanic* and the iceberg, our worlds were destined to collide, unless we could figure out a way to stop them. A fresh tremor shook the garden.

"How long d'you reckon we've got?" asked Zack, steadying himself in the aftermath.

The shadow slid another degree across the face of the sun, and I had my answer to Zack's question. It wasn't a convenient flaming countdown in the sky, but the next best thing. "I'm betting the universes will crash together at total eclipse." I swallowed thickly. "When the light goes out, the lights go out."

Lara grabbed her notepad and began making calculations, quickly and neatly filling two pages with numbers. "Then using the rate at which the sun is disappearing, I estimate that impact will occur in a little over…" She paused. "Twenty-two minutes."

I set a timer on her counterpart's phone and turned to my brother. What we faced was far beyond my capabilities – I was hoping he had the solution. "Zack, can you stop them?"

"No chance. My powers are barely at thirty per cent and even fully charged, giant asteroids are one thing – this is on a cosmic scale."

The dark boundary of a storm front slid overhead. Lightning lanced from billowing black clouds and a crack of thunder split the sky. In the face of the apocalypse, the weather was going haywire. Another rumble. For a second I thought it was more thunder, but then I realised it was coming from the tree house. I snapped my head round to see Stellar, tied to the chair, blast through the roof like a fighter pilot in an ejector seat.

"But how?" mumbled a dumbfounded Zack.

"Rocket shoes." I pointed at the twin jets of fire pouring from the heels of his school brogues. He must have held on to them after they appeared in my bedroom.

Once more I felt a sneaking sense of admiration.

Stellar manoeuvred himself away from the influence of the superpower-sapping cats and shrugged off his restraints. Discarded ropes and bits of broken chair tumbled to earth, landing with a crash in the crater made by Nemesis. He hovered above us, rocket shoes belching flame.

"Stellar, you have to listen to me," I pleaded. "At total eclipse the world is going to—"

"Blah blah blah." He cut across me. "Save your breath, Other Luke. The world is *not* ending. It's just a trick to make me give up Zack. Well, forget it. He's staying here with me."

He was deluded.

"No," said Zack calmly and firmly. "Luke and I are leaving. Together."

"Oh yeah, and how d'you figure that, when I have *this*?" Stellar stuck out a hand and curled his fingers in a beckoning motion. For maximum effect, something evil ought to have happened immediately, but it didn't.

Nothing continued to happen.

He looked faintly embarrassed, hovering there, one rigid arm shaking with the effort of whatever it was he was trying to do. "I would've brought it with me," he said cryptically, "but I wasn't expecting to be turned into the *Purr-isoner of Azkaban*."

The terrible cat-pun effect lingered like old kitty litter. We waited some more.

"Are you using telekinesis to bring something here from a great distance?" I enquired.

"Maybe," Stellar said cagily.

"But not from another universe? Because then you'd use a gerbil-hole."

He scowled. "It's in my bedroom, if you must know."

"Is it a weapon?"

"Look, I'm not playing Supervillain Twenty Questions. Ah, here it comes." The relief in his voice was evident.

An object whistled out of the sky and landed with a smack in his open palm. It was a blue-painted metal cube layered with glass. I remembered that I'd seen it before, on the roof of Dad's comic shop, just before Stellar took Zack. Back then Stellar had called it a loose end. With a cough from his rocket shoes he flew down to the ground, held out the object and let go. I caught it in both hands.

"Oof!" It was a lot heavier than it looked.

"In case you were thinking that S.C.A.R.F. is coming to your rescue," he said with an unsettling smile.

A deep-noted chime sounded from within the cube. I dropped it in shock. It hit the ground, wobbled once and came to rest on one side. With horror I realised what it was.

"*Zorbon's interdimensional craft.*"

Stellar had used his powers to squish it into a paperweight.

"You honestly thought I'd leave behind the one thing that could ruin my plan?" He looked offended. "I mean, really, what do you take me for?"

Once more I'd been outmanoeuvred by my Evil Twin. And right then, staring into his smug face – *my* smug face – something in me snapped. With a howl of fury I charged at him. I wasn't expecting to breach his superpowered defences, and evidently neither was he. I took him by surprise, tackling him to the ground. He landed heavily, gasping for breath. I'd knocked the wind out of him. But my victory was temporary. With a snarl, he launched himself at me, crushing me in a bear hug. We rolled over and over across the garden.

I could hear Zack shouting at us to stop, Serge encouraging me to punch Stellar on the nose and Lara yelling out the countdown.

"Sixteen minutes to apocalypse!"

"Enough!" cried Zack. "Quit it, right now. Don't make me pull you two apart."

The phrase rang round my head. *Pull us apart.*

Of course.

I stopped fighting. It took Stellar another few seconds before he realised I was no longer resisting, and then he stopped too.

"Had enough?" he said, straightening his cape.

I barely heard him. I had made a decision – the most difficult of my life. I ought to have been scared but instead I was flooded with a sense of calm. We disentangled ourselves and got to our feet.

"Don't try anything funny," warned Stellar.

I shook my head. There was nothing funny about what I had to do. "We were never meant to meet, for a lot of reasons. One being that when we're together we generate a super-powerful magnetic field." He looked at me blankly. "Don't you see – it's us? *We're* pulling our universes together." My throat was dry. "Even if you won't let Zack go, you have to send me back to my world."

Superman's dad sent him away because their world was dying. Jor-El didn't want to leave his son alone in the universe, but he had no other choice. Now I had to go, to save my world. Even if it meant leaving Zack behind.

"No way," said Zack. "Absolutely not happening."

"Zack, listen to me, if I don't leave in the next –" I glanced at Lara.

"Thirteen minutes," she confirmed.

"– then it's the end for all of us."

Zack wrung his hands. "There must be another way." But he knew there wasn't. "Luke, no." And in the tone of his voice I could hear that he'd accepted my decision.

I couldn't remember if I'd ever properly looked at my big brother's face. Who does that? It would be weird. But at that moment I didn't want to take my eyes off him. I knew that when I did finally turn away, it would be for the last time.

"At least this way I'll know you're alive." I swallowed. This was proving harder than I'd believed possible. "Even if it's in another universe." I fought to hold back tears. I knew that if I started to cry, I might never stop. I swung round to face Stellar. "Now. Do it now!"

He hesitated.

"Stellar, please," I pleaded. I daren't look back at my brother.

"It really is the end of the world, isn't it?" Stellar said quietly. He sat down heavily on the ground and clasped his hands to his head. "I wish… I wish I'd never been given superpowers. I wish *I* was the one who'd left the tree house that night. Then he'd still be alive." He looked up at Zack and when he did something in his face had changed. Anguish was replaced with acceptance.

"I'll send you home," he said. "Both of you."

I daren't believe it. "It's a trick. Has to be."

"Not necessarily," said Serge. "There are many examples of supervillains who experience a change of heart and cross to the Light Side. For example, Black Widow, Rogue and Emma Frost."

"All women," grumbled Lara.

"For what I've done I deserve to be alone," said Stellar.

"No. You don't," said Lara. "And you're not. You've got me."

Serge took a step forward and extended a hand. "*Et moi.*"

Stellar clasped Serge's hand and got to his feet. He walked to the centre of the garden and raised his arms; a maestro preparing to conduct his cosmic symphony.

"He's doing it." I couldn't conceal my amazement. "He's actually going to save us."

"Of course he is," said Zack. "He's you. More or less."

"Wait!" cried Lara. "What if this is the gerbil-hole that triggers—"

"The Emmental apocalypse," Serge finished.

Really, still with the cheese thing? This wasn't the time to get into an argument. "We don't have a choice."

Stellar began his efforts. He made a circling motion with one hand, summoning the gerbil-hole into existence. We held our breath, scanning the sky, waiting for a sight of the by now familiar phenomenon. We were still holding our breath fifteen seconds later. Not a sausage. Or indeed a chip. During the battle with Zack, Stellar had created multiple holes in the blink of an eye, so what was taking so long?

Judging from his puzzled expression, the same question had occurred to Stellar. He began again, redoubling his efforts, straining to create the portal that would take us home and save our worlds. With a shout of frustration he turned to us.

"I can't do it. I'm out of power. The cats, the fight. Nothing left." His shoulders slumped.

That was not what any of us wanted to hear.

The shadow of our universe continued its relentless slide across the surface of the fast-disappearing sun. Time was almost up.

"Per'aps we could give him a boost?" suggested Serge.

"There isn't enough sunlight to recharge him," said Lara, glancing into the sky.

"And by the time I've flown him into space for a dose of starlight, it'll be too late," said Zack grimly.

I snapped my fingers. "What about your charger?"

"How long have we got?" he said.

"About eight minutes," said Lara.

Zack shook his head. Not enough.

There was a rumble, as if two thunder-gods were fighting over the remote control. A tremor shook the ground – the most powerful yet – throwing us across the garden. I struggled to stay on my feet as the quake split open the earth. Like a crack in a collapsing wall, it zigzagged across the garden. Its ragged course brushed my toes and I found myself teetering on the edge of a deep crevasse. The hole gaped like Gordon the World-Eater's lipless mouth. Dizzy at the drop I took a step back. The loose soil gave way under me, I lost my footing and fell.

30
THE BOY WHO WOULDN'T GROW UP

I plunged down the side of the muddy chasm, bouncing off exposed rocks and tree roots, desperately clawing at the walls as I fell into darkness. At last I felt my fingers dig in to the mud and I slithered to a stop. Clods of loose earth tumbled around my ears. I had no idea how far I'd fallen. I daren't look down. I was hanging on, but only just. Above me I heard the others yelling my name.

"I'm OK," I shouted.

"I'm coming, Luke," Zack's voice sounded in my head. "I still have some power left."

Power. Of course. It was so obvious, why hadn't I thought of it before? "Zack, no! Don't waste it."

"What?!"

"Stop using telepathy," I called out. "You're going to need every drop of your powers." I began the slow and painful climb back to the surface. "You and Stellar have to do it together," I shouted, hauling myself up on tree roots. "Combine your forces to create the gerbil-hole."

"Got it," Zack shouted in reply.

All I could do was get back to the surface in time, the rest was up to Zack and Stellar. I daren't put a foot wrong. One slip, one fall, and it would all be over.

Above me I glimpsed the last remnants of daylight, and against the fading light a silhouette. It took me a few seconds to realise what I was looking at. Lara and Serge had formed a human chain. Serge's arms were wrapped around Lara's legs. She hung over the edge of the drop like a bat.

I scrambled up the slippery wall of mud, eyes fixed on her outstretched hands.

"I see him!" she cried, stretching towards me.

I reached out. Our fingertips brushed – once, twice. I felt my footing slip. I threw myself at her.

And missed.

As I fell back, I made one last desperate attempt and seized the cuff of her jumper. I was hanging on by a thread.

There was a slap as her other hand clamped my wrist.

"Got you!" she shouted. "Serge, pull!"

The two of them groaned as they bore my weight. Sliding and scrabbling, they hauled me back up to the garden. I flopped on the ground beside my exhausted friends, but our relief was short-lived.

A cold wind howled through the oak tree. All that remained of the sky was a splinter of daylight like a crack in a closing door. The end was approaching fast.

A cry of frustration joined the shriek of the wind. Zack and Stellar stood in front of the tree house. They had joined hands in an attempt to combine their powers, but so far with no success.

Zack dropped Stellar's hand. "I can't... I don't know what I'm doing."

"Try again," said my twin, slipping his hand in Zack's once more. "You can do it."

Zack nodded, took several deep breaths and pulled himself together. "OK. Think of home. Mum and Dad. Physics tutoring with Cara. GCSEs."

He tried again.

"Come on, Zack," I urged under my breath.

"Home. Home," he repeated. "There's no place like home." But nothing appeared. Not the glimmer of a gerbil-hole.

My plan wasn't working.

Behind us came the sound of scraping metal. Pushing aside the fence panels was the figure of Cara Lee. She crossed the garden with a dazed expression, almost as if she was sleepwalking.

"Uh, what are you doing here?" asked Lara.

Cara barely registered her sister's presence. Her eyes were fixed on Zack. "I was at school," she mumbled. "We were streaming the superhero fight. Then I got home and saw lights in the garden..." She tailed off and turned to me. "The other night, at dinner. All that stuff you said about a parallel world. I have these dreams. Ever since it happened. Zack's there, but in them he's ... flying." It was hard to see in the fading light, but I think she was crying.

"Cara," mumbled Zack.

She placed a hand on his cheek. "Zack."

Normally when my brother is around Cara he stutters or walks into furniture. Thankfully there wasn't a chest of drawers in the garden and just as it looked as if he was about to say more, she leaned in and kissed him.

"French fries!" shouted Serge. "I smell the French fries!"

A swirling gerbil-hole bloomed in the darkening sky.

Stellar and Zack (with a snog from Cara) had done it!

"Two minutes and counting," said Lara. "It's going to be close."

"Uh-oh, something is emerging from the hole," said Serge.

An outline began to form in the mouth of the dimensional portal. Swiftly, it took shape. Not a gerbil with laser-eyes, nor rocket shoes, nor a world-eating destroyer. Something far less impossible, but unexpected just the same.

A bus.

It sailed through the sky and fell to earth, landing hard on the other side of the fence. Somehow its suspension survived the descent. Headlights raking the garden, it crashed through the fence, slid across the grass gouging out two deep tracks, and with a squeal of brakes stopped centimetres from the crevasse. The engine idled noisily.

I registered the number on the destination board above the cab. This wasn't just any bus.

"The 227," I muttered.

My bus home.

With a hiss the front doors opened. I turned to the others. I wanted to say something, but a frantic Lara cut me off.

"What are you waiting for?!" she yelled, pushing me towards the door. "Get on the flipping bus!"

"Au revoir, mes amis." Serge waved us goodbye. *"Vite.* Quickly!"

"I'll miss you," Cara whispered to Zack.

"Zack…" Stellar threw himself into my brother's arms.

Looking back, I'm not sure who let go of whom first, but the hug came to an end. Zack leapt aboard the bus and, as the doors began to close, Stellar laid a hand on the glass and mouthed something. Zack was close enough to hear, but I couldn't make it out.

In comics no one ever really dies. At least not permanently. They almost always come back in another issue. But for Stellar there would always be a Zack-shaped hole in the universe. At least this time he got a chance to say goodbye.

The wheels of the bus spun, struggling for traction, and then bit. Instead of heading across the garden, the nose rose straight up and we lifted off, bearing for the gerbil-hole. Thrown off balance by the violent ascent, Zack and I were pitched backwards. With a yell we slid the length of the aisle to the very back of the bus. Through the rear window the last thing I saw of the Other World was Stellar, in full flight behind us. For a moment I thought he was about to follow the bus, but as we crossed over he stopped at the boundary, watching.

He began to wave. Zack and I knelt up on the seats and waved back. Stellar hovered there, a sad smile on his face.

The gerbil-hole closed behind us and the bus shot forward. Instantly, I felt the gap between our universes widen.

I turned to Zack. "What did he say to you?"

He propped his head in his hands and stared out of the window. "Second star to the right, and straight on till morning."

31
ALL CHANGE

I could feel our universes separate, the space between them expanding rapidly as I left Stellar behind. The previous time I'd travelled through a gerbil-hole I'd emerged instantly on the other side. This time it was clear we were in for a lengthier journey. We steered past planets and suns, bypassed a supernova and did a three-point turn to avoid a Black Hole. I caught my reflection in the darkened window. I barely recognised myself. I looked ... relieved. And then it hit me that I was going home. I glanced at Zack. *We* were going home. For one perfect moment I felt a glow of satisfaction – and then I remembered Stellar.

"You OK?" said Zack. He was watching me from his seat. Since our brief exchange after departing Other Bromley, the journey had passed in sombre silence.

I nodded. "How about you?"

"I kissed Cara," he said dreamily.

"Technically, she wasn't your Cara," I pointed out. Last month Zack had kissed an alien cyborg Cara, today a parallel version of her. This was becoming a habit.

"I have a girlfriend," he said in the same faraway voice.

"Yeah," I mumbled. "In another dimension."

He gave me a hard stare.

"Uh, who's driving the bus?" I asked, keen to change the subject.

"No one's driving it," he said, adding unconvincingly, "It's, y'know, quantum physics."

Like that ever explained anything. "So who's wearing the hat?"

In the driver's compartment, reflected in the large rear-view mirror, sat a figure in a peaked cap. As I asked the question, the figure lifted his head, revealing his face.

"Zorbon!" Zack gasped.

"The Decider?"

"No, the Dentist." He rolled his eyes.

We made our way forward. Before me, finally, was Zorbon the Decider: representative of the High

Council of Frodax Wonthreen Rrr'n'fargh, Bestower of Superpowers upon the Unworthy, Prophet of Doom when it Comes to Things Like Giant Asteroids and Evil Gym Teachers, The One Who Always Shows Up When I'm in the Toilet. He wore a high-collared purple cape, and I could just make out a collection of stars glowing on his chest. He was just as Zack had described him, with one crucial detail left out. His head barely rose above the level of the wheel.

"He's teeny-tiny," I whispered. "Give him a fishing rod, you could hire him out as a garden gnome."

Zack scowled.

"YOU DID WELL," Zorbon's voice boomed. It was like hearing thunder from a squeaky bath duck.

I raised a questioning finger. "Uh, just to be clear, Mr Zorbon, Your Honour. First off, Hello. Nice to meet you. *Finally*. Uh, so my question is this. *Who* did well? Is your praise only for Star Lad, or am I included too? And if so, is there a reward? Y'know, because if you're giving out superpowers, I have a list. I've been thinking about it. A lot."

"Luke!" Zack hissed. "You can't ask for superpowers. That's not how it works."

"Says who?"

Zack gave me a pitying look. I realised with dismay

279

that it was the same look I used to give him whenever he asked a stupid question about Green Lantern's ring powers, or the limits of Superman's strength. He was right, of course. The comic tables had well and truly turned.

"Zorbon, I think this is yours," said Zack, handing him the squished interdimensional craft the size of a large bar of Dairy Milk.

"HMM." Zorbon inspected the damage. "THAT WILL BUFF OUT." He rubbed a corner of the ship with his sleeve. "NOW, TAKE YOUR SEATS." He swung the steering wheel and Zack and I were thrown on top of each other. "WE ARE COMING IN TO LAND." There was a crunch of gears as he shifted down. "BRACE YOURSELVES!"

One moment we were whizzing through the folds of space, the next the bus crashed down on an ordinary and very familiar road. The suspension groaned in protest, tyres shrieked as we skidded on the wrong side towards an oncoming car. Shocked by the sudden appearance of the 227, the driver swerved out of the way, blaring his horn. Zorbon regained control and we slowed to a much more bus-like trundle.

It was then that I noticed something weird. Zorbon had grown. And not like a centimetre or two – this was magic beanstalk stuff. His hat brushed the roof of the driver's compartment. It seemed that travelling through the quantum realm could do strange things to a person.

"Look," said Zack, pointing.

The sun hung low over the rooftops, perfect and round. There was no sign of the shadow universe.

"Did we…?"

"YES," replied Zorbon, without hearing the whole question. He had a habit of knowing the end before it happened.

We'd saved the world, the universe, the multiverse. The whole big shebang. And I needed a rest.

"We're home," I said. Something in my voice sounded strange, but I put it down to the excitement of the moment.

Grinning with relief, Zack turned to me. The grin vanished from his face. But much more worrying than the loss of the grin was the face. It wasn't his.

"Luke?"

"Zack?" That voice again. Although it was coming out of my mouth, it wasn't *mine*.

Slowly we both looked up into the mirror hanging over the driver's compartment. Our horrified reflections gazed back down at us. Something had happened in the journey between universes. Something terrible.

We'd changed.

He was me.

And I was my brother.

Ding! The bus bell chimed. This was our stop.

ACKNOWLEDGEMENTS

I was about to write my customary thank-you note when the following document arrived via a gerbil-hole. It appears to be written by a version of me from an alternate universe.

I, Citizen Author number 451 of the Independent Publishing State of North Crowea, offer my humble and insufficient thanks to our glorious ruler in perpetuity, Supreme Leader Wilson. I present my poorly parsed gratitude to First Minister Stansfield. This book would not exist without her benevolent, sleep-depriving supervision. I am uneasily indebted to the Head of Brainwashing, Minister Stokes, and her feared emissaries from the Department of Propaganda, Vice-Chairman Kingston and Director Hall-Craggs.

I express ballistic appreciation to Marshal Gotkowska of the Overseas Secretariat for her long-range global strategy. My terrified thanks to Section Bounce of our revered Secret Police, for their tireless work twisting arms and infiltrating bookshops. Once again I marvel at the skills of citizens Laura Ellen Anderson, Rob Biddulph and Robin Boyden (state-approved illustrators numbers 16, 17 and 18), in abject collaboration with Head of the Design Dungeons, Director Theobald. Strict, hierarchical thanks to the rest of the Central Committee, including Minister Bonnick and Deputy Scoble.

I acknowledge that I would not be where I am without Agent Stan. And if anyone can hear me, please send help.

Finally, to my life partner and brood mother of our 18 children, Natasha, see, I have obtained the correct permit for another child! Why are you running away like that…?

★★★